An Unforeseen Love 2

**Lock Down Publications and Ca$h
Presents
An Unforeseen Love 2
A Novel by *Meesha***

Lock Down Publications
Po Box 944
Stockbridge, Ga 30281

Visit our website @
www.lockdownpublications.com

Copyright 2021 by Meesha
An Unforeseen Love 2

First Edition October 2021
Printed in the United States of America

This is a work of fiction. Names, characters, places, and incidents either are products of the author's imagination or are used fictitiously. Any similarity to actual events or locales or persons, living or dead, is entirely coincidental.

Lock Down Publications
Like our page on Facebook: Lock Down Publications @
www.facebook.com/lockdownpublications.ldp
Book interior design by: **Shawn Walker**
Edited by: **Jill Alicea**

Meesha

Stay Connected with Us!

Text **LOCKDOWN** to 22828 to stay up-to-date with new releases,
sneak peaks, contests and more…
Thank you.

Submission Guideline.

Submit the first three chapters of your completed manuscript to ldpsubmissions@gmail.com, subject line: Your book's title. The manuscript must be in a .doc file and sent as an attachment. Document should be in Times New Roman, double spaced and in size 12 font. Also, provide your synopsis and full contact information. If sending multiple submissions, they must each be in a separate email.

Have a story but no way to send it electronically? You can still submit to LDP/Ca$h Presents. Send in the first three chapters, written or typed, of your completed manuscript to:

LDP: Submissions Dept
Po Box 944
Stockbridge, Ga 30281

DO NOT send original manuscript. Must be a duplicate.

Provide your synopsis and a cover letter containing your full contact information.

Thanks for considering LDP and Ca$h Presents.

Dedication

This book is dedicated to anyone that is struggling with drug abuse or knows of someone that's fighting addiction. One thing that many need to understand is, people that are dealing with any type of addiction didn't choose to be an addict. There are many different reasons and circumstances that leads them in that direction. Love and support are two of the main factors that are needed in the situation. You may not agree with the lifestyle they lead, but knowing they're not alone is what they need at times. Every day they're beating themselves up for falling to the lowest of the low. It's up to them to want change. It can't be forced upon them. It's a waste of time until they are ready to do what's right. Beating them down won't change anything. Keep the love strong and earn their trust. Eventually, they will reach out for help, Then again, maybe they won't. But never turn your back, because addicts need love too.

You are the Reason
Calum Scott

There goes my heart beating
'Cause you are the reason
I'm losing my sleep
Please come back now

And there goes my mind racing
And you are the reason
That I'm still breathing
I'm hopeless now

I'd climb every mountain
And swim every ocean
Just to be with you
And fix what I've broken
Oh, 'cause I need you to see
That you are the reason

There goes my hand shaking
And you are the reason
My heart keeps bleeding
I need you now

And if I could turn back the clock
I'd make sure the light defeated the dark
I'd spend every hour of every day
Keeping you safe

And I'd climb every mountain
And swim every ocean
Just to be with you
And fix what I've broken
Oh, 'cause I need to see you
That you are the reason, oh

(I don't wanna fight no more)
(I don't wanna hurt no more)
(I don't wanna cry no more)
(Come back, I need you to hold me closer now)
You are the reason, Oh
(Just a little closer now)
(Come a little closer now)
(I need to hold me tonight)

I'd climb every mountain
And swim any ocean
Just to be with you
And fix what I've broken
'Cause I need you to see
That you are the reason

Meesha

Chapter 1

The past couple weeks were filled with fun, laughter, and plenty of drama. With all the things Chade and Ahmad endured, Malik knew time was winding down for his shit show to begin. He hadn't spoken to Ailani since finding out about her sneaky ass and the nigga she'd been creeping with. Malik's phone hadn't stopped ringing with her name appearing on the screen, but he refused to answer. Utilizing the vacation days he'd accumulated was a must to get his head back in the game, and Malik opted to spend that time with Toni in Chicago.

Being in her element gave them the opportunity to see where the relationship could go from that point on. Malik could honestly say, he was loving her hospitality. Toni was a round the way girl with the professionalism of a woman that wasn't going to allow the negativity of life stand in the way of her achieving the goals she set in play for herself. While she worked, Malik stayed at her home and chilled. When Toni walked in from a long day of work, dinner would be waiting for her along with a bath and a full body massage.

Chade's proposal to Baylei came as a surprise to everyone because he fought tooth and nail to prevent himself from catching feelings for any woman. Baylei was a special type of woman and she had Mr. Lover Man wrapped around her finger. Malik always thought he would be the next man in line to say "I do", but things changed all the way around when Ahmad didn't walk down the aisle in St. Thomas. It was like the movie *Final Destination*; that shit skipped to the next person. Instead of people dying, muthafuckas were falling head over heels for the ones they were destined to be with.

As Malik walked into the brick home his father had purchased through a friend of his, he took a deep breath with a smile. Miss Teresa did her thang when she found and presented the property to his father. It was a little too much for a single man, but it was going to be phenomenal whenever he decided to settle down with the woman he would grow to love.

What he had with Toni was new and Malik didn't want to jinx anything by saying they were going to be together for the long haul. Seeing as how the two of them lived thousands of miles away from one another, it was going to take lots of trust and commitment to get to the point of even speaking on love. Malik had nothing but time, but what he did know was that he was feeling the hell out of the woman he was smitten with in St. Thomas.

He was going to have to settle the situation with Ailani first and foremost. Bringing the unfinished business hanging in the air was something he didn't want to do, because it would cause more problems to come between what he was trying to build with Toni. But Malik knew he would have to dissolve it for his own well-being also. The toxicity of not addressing the issue with Ailani wasn't healthy for either one of them.

The hardwood floors shined under Malik's feet as he walked from room to room admiring the layout. The furniture, appliances, and everything else were very homely and he loved every bit of it. Without his parents, especially his mother, Malik would've walked into an empty house. After having a heart to heart with both of his parents, they agreed to help him relocate in order for him to get his life back on track.

Malik Daniels Sr. was pissed when his son told him about the things Ailani had put him through. Malik was embarrassed because he thought he looked like a sucka in his father's eyes. But when his father reassured him that everyone got the wool pulled over their eyes at least once in their lifetime, he felt better about his situation. Malik's father made him promise to leave Ailani alone for good because she was no good for him. That was easy to do because he was done with her long before he told them what happened.

His mother, Jeanette, wanted to go to Malik's other home and kick Ailani's ass. To calm her down, Malik assured her of the eviction process he started while in Chicago. He was already three steps ahead to remove Ailani from the premises, then he would put the house up for sale.

As Malik walked into the kitchen, the granite countertops and stainless-steel appliances had the room looking as if it belonged in a magazine. Opening cabinets and the refrigerator, Malik shook his head because his mother made sure he was straight on the grocery side.

Hiking the strap of his bag on his shoulder, Malik roamed the lower level of the house as he continued his walk-through. There was a laundry room next to a bathroom and between a bedroom and a small linen closet. He passed a door he suspected was the entry to the basement and wanted to save that space for a later date. Malik had plans to turn that area into his mancave. As he headed up the steps, his phone rang in his pocket and he rushed to retrieve it.

Slowly walking upward, Malik smiled at the sight of a picture of Toni which appeared on the screen. Tapping the green button to connect the call, Malik pushed the speaker button. "Hey, you."

"Hello, handsome. I wanted to make sure you got back to Cali safely." Malik could hear the smile in her voice and it warmed his heart.

"Yeah, I did. I'm walking through the new house now," he said, making his way to the top of the landing. "It's a lot of space for one man, but I'll make it work for me. How was your day?"

"My day was soothing. I did some cleaning and now I'm relaxing. You have my home feeling as if it's missing something since you left this afternoon."

"You better stop mackin', girl. Acting like you missing a nigga and shit." Malik laughed as he entered what he was sure was the master bedroom.

The décor screamed masculinity and he knew his father was the person that decked the room out for him. There was a big California king-sized bed in the middle of the room with matching dressers and nightstands. The black and grey color scheme was to his liking and the fact that there were blackout curtains at the windows were a plus. Malik hated when the sun beamed into his face first thing in the morning.

"I'm not mackin'." Toni laughed. "It's just having you here with me was a pleasure. Now, I have to figure out who's going to have my dinner ready when I get home in the evenings since you left me."

"Yo' ass better prep that shit the night before because bet' not no other nigga attempt to do the things that has your ass spoiled. That's my damn job, woman. It would be nothing for me to do a fly-by. You will never know when I'll be back in Chicago. I left some property there that I will have to check on sooner rather than later."

"Property? What kind of property did you purchase while here and why didn't you tell me about your investment?" Toni curiously asked.

"Well, I didn't actually *buy* anything. I just put in the time with a woman and her private parts. I conformed the pussy to get wet only when I'm around."

Toni laughed loudly as if what Malik said was a joke. He put his bag on the bed and hit the end button on his phone and placed it on the nightstand. Malik undressed, putting his clothes in the hamper that sat by the closet when his phone rang with a Facetime call from Toni. Laughing out loud, he allowed the phone to ring to the very end before he answered.

"Malik, don't ever hang up on me! What was that about?" Toni asked with a scowl on her face.

"When you feel what I say is a joke, I don't take to that very well. But, I'm back with you now," he smirked. "You care to inform me of why you laughed at me?"

"I didn't laugh *at* you, I laughed at what you said. My pussy only does what I want it to do. It has nothing to do with you or anyone else."

"Is that right?" Malik asked as he laid back on his bed and lowered the phone.

With his joint in his hand, he stroked it slowly while gazing into Toni's eyes from afar. Turning the camera around so Toni could see what he was doing, Malik watched her mouth gape slightly as she focused on the movements of his hand. A small sliver of drool slid out the corner of her mouth and Malik chuckled.

"Let me see that pussy, Toni. I want you to see for yourself that even if I'm not with you physically, your lady parts are going to react to my presence."

"My—my—my pussy is desert dry over here," she stuttered.

"Why are you nervous? The sight of this *dick* got you over there fumbling the ball. Put that thang in my face Toni."

"I'm not about to do this with you, Malik," Toni said, rolling her eyes.

Malik decided to please himself while she was on the phone to see her reaction. Stroking his pipe slowly, he got up and went into the bathroom in search of some lubricant. When he found a jar of Vaseline, he took it back to his bedroom and got comfortable on the bed. Malik got back up and went to the linen closet for a towel. Once he placed it on the bed, he was ready to get his shit off.

"What are you doing, Malik?" Toni asked.

"I'm getting acquainted with my girlfriend. Do you mind?" he laughed.

"Your girlfriend?"

"Yep. I'll introduce y'all in a few minutes." Malik picked up the phone and smiled at Toni but she didn't find anything funny. As a matter of fact, the frown on her face was deeper than the ocean waters they enjoyed in St. Thomas. "Okay, I'm back. Why are you muggin' me, bae?"

"Don't question me! Show me this damn girlfriend of yours."

Malik reached over and grabbed the Vaseline from the nightstand. Bringing the object into the camera, Toni laughed until she had tears streaming down her face. The sight of the lubrication was funny as hell, but she was low-key glad it was Vaseline and not a woman.

"Toni, meet my number one bitch, Vassi. She's going to keep me company if this long-distance shit has any chance of working. Isn't she beautiful?"

"Something is wrong with you. What the hell you about to do with that?"

"I can show you better than I can tell you, but first, you must come out ya clothes," Malik smirked.

"I've never had video sex before, Malik. I'd rather wait until we see one another in person. This isn't for me, sorry."

"Take off your clothes, Antonia Wade. I want to see that glossy slit that had my mouth watering before I devoured it with my tongue," Malik demanded lowly. "The smell of peaches is filling my nostrils and ain't shit fruity around this damn house. That's you taking me back to your essence where I wanna be."

Toni propped her phone on the dresser as she pointed the remote toward the television. The sounds of "High for This" by The Weeknd blared through the surround system. She started gyrating her hips and Malik's member swelled in his hand as he watched her every move. Taking the lid off the Vaseline, he palmed a nice amount and caressed his pipe slowly.

Malik watched as Toni pulled her shirt over her head and slowly eased the shorts she wore over her voluptuous hips. The plumpness of her ass had him thinking about the sex session they had earlier that morning. Toni bent over and ran her fingers over her thick mound and just as he thought, it was wet for him. Climbing on top of her bed, Malik had a full view of her honey pot. Placing the earbud in her left ear, Toni inserted her finger into her mouth before rubbing her nub slowly.

"Yeah, get her right for me, baby." Malik said lowly. "Stick your finger in that muthafucka and picture me pleasing yo' sexy ass."

Toni purred like a kitten arching her back. Reaching under her pillow, she came out with her vibrator and the sound alone had her smiling.

"Make her cum for me."

She turned the gadget on the highest speed and went to town. The sight before him had Malik wishing he would've stayed right there with Toni, knowing she was about to erupt like a volcano. The fuck faces she made as the vibrations hummed on her clit had Malik ready to catch a flight in spite of having to work the next day. A slight moan from her throat and the way her back elevated off the bed let him know she was at the peak of eruption.

"Yeah, baby. That pussy taste good as hell. You like the way my tongue feels on that clit, don't you?"

Toni closed her eyes and the image that displayed behind her lids took her back to the hotel in St. Thomas. Malik was positioned between her legs like a sniper eyeing its next target. The way he studied her lady parts, she knew he was about to murder the prey. When his soft tongue glided along her slit, a shiver slid down her spine in anticipation of his next move. Malik wrapped his lips around her bud and that was all he wrote.

"Yes, Malik! Eat this pussy," Toni moaned as her head turned from side to side. "Right there! I'm about to cum!"

"You bet' not! I want to shoot up yo' spot as your pussy grip my shit. I'm almost there with you though."

Malik stroked his joint slowly as he watched Toni struggling hard to hold her climax. The way the white cum slid down the crack of her ass had his nut rushing to the finish line. The way she thrusted around was sexy and he wanted to see her squirt for only him to see. Breathing rapidly, a grunt escaped Malik's lips but his eyes stayed trained on the beautiful picture before him. Toni's moans filled his bedroom.

"Cum with me, baby!"

Both of their sounds of pleasure would've interrupted all in ear-shot if they hadn't been alone. Toni didn't disappoint when the flood of her juices shot from her bud. The endless flow of her discretions was beautiful and Malik couldn't stop the creamy filling that sprouted from the head of his dick. Moving his hand up and down a few more times, he smiled as he came down from the high he was on.

"You are one nasty muthafucka." Toni laughed as she placed her toy beside her. "I'm gonna have so much fun with this newfound obsession. Thank you."

"Damn, bae. Your pussy cried a river over there," Malik laughed. "That bed fucked up, but that shit is sexy as fuck!"

"Stop playing, acting like you don't know. Ain't shit but tsunamis over here. You know firsthand because you almost got wiped out on more than one occasion."

"Toni, you gon' get locked up for manslaughter one day. That shit is deadly, and guess what? I'm down with all that nasty shit. I can't wait to drink every drop of your sweet nectar." Toni stifled a yawn and that was Malik's cue to get off the phone. "Take a nap, baby. I put your ass to sleep without putting a hand on you. I'm not gon' front though, you did the same over here too, ma."

Toni smiled as she maneuvered to the dry side of her bed. Yawning again, she didn't even have a rebuttal to what he said. That further let Malik know she was about to be out for the count. "Okay. I'll call you when I wake up," Toni said, turning onto her side.

Malik watched as her chest fell slowly and her breathing labored. He watched her a few more minutes before ending the call. Stifling a yawn of his own, Malik got up to clean himself up. As much as he wanted to snooze, he had things to do before jumping back into work.

After getting out of the shower, thoughts of Toni entered his mind. Those thoughts were short-lived when his phone rang and Ailani's name appeared on the screen. Not wanting to prolong the inevitable, Malik finally answered the call he'd been dreading. Before he could say hello after the call connected, Ailani was going off on him.

"Why the fuck you haven't been answering your phone? You've been back from your so-called vacation for weeks, Malik. Why haven't I seen or heard from you?" Malik rubbed his body with coconut oil as he listened to Ailani rant without interruption. She looked down at the phone to make sure he hadn't hung up. "Are you fucking listening to me?"

"I'm listening," Malik answered nonchalantly. "My question to you is, are you finished?"

"What you mean am I finished? You haven't answered not one of the questions I've asked! You owe me—"

"Let me stop you there, Ailani. I don't owe you shit. I've sat back and let you talk shit about things that hold no weight with me. For years, you manipulated me and I was blinded by the fake love you were always stressing you had for a nigga. The way you ran through my bread and hid that shit was foul in itself, but I'm over that shit."

Malik walked to his closet and retrieved a pair of denim shorts and I crisp white tee. He went to the dresser and took out a pair of socks and boxers before sitting back on the end of his bed. He took a deep breath because he felt the anger building as he talked to Ailani.

"How about we talk about the shit you're not trying to speak on. All that other shit is irrelevant to me."

"I don't know what you're talking about. Enlighten me and stop talking in circles, Malik."

"Oh, I'm coming right out with my shit. Hopefully you ready to tell the truth about the matter. How long have you been seeing the nigga you were parading around with while I was gone?"

Ailani was silent, trying to come up with a lie fast enough to appease him, but it didn't work in her favor.

"Don't get quiet now. What, the cat got your tongue now? You had so much to say a few minutes ago and the diarrhea was on a steady flow coming from your mouth. Where's all that tough shit now, Ailani? Keep that shit funky, ma. I want the same energy you had when you harped on my line when I picked up."

Malik was pissed and her silence only made matters worse. Continuing to dress, he slipped his feet in his sneakers and shook his head as put on his fitted cap. He slipped his wallet in his pocket and grabbed his keys before picking his phone up from the bed. Pressing the end button, Malik disconnected the call and headed out the door.

"Fuck Ailani. The bitch don't have to explain shit to me. She's a done deal," he said as he made it to the bottom of the stairs and left the house.

Meesha

Chapter 2

Toni was sitting behind her desk, looking over the case file that was opened in front of her. Jasper Kaminski was in for a treat with the case he took on. It was obvious that the client was guilty as fuck, but that was none of Toni's business. She was baffled at the things she'd read but she had to remember, that wasn't what she got paid to do. Her job was to organize the documents, and prepare the affidavits. All the other shit was up to the folks that would be representing the dirty bastard. Toni could already feel the headache she would have while discussing the case in a whole.

Taking her reading glasses from her face, she rubbed a hand down her face and glanced at the clock on the wall. It was eleven-thirty. That gave her thirty minutes before she was scheduled to meet Baylei and Jordyn for lunch. The break was truly needed because her morning had been a busy one. Her phone pinged and she didn't hesitate to see who the text was from. A smile appeared on her face the minute she saw Malik's name.

She hadn't talked to him other than a few texts here and there since the day of their video session. It wasn't purposely done, but she had been busy as hell and basically fell out the minute she arrived home most nights. Being tired was an understatement, Toni was "tied" at the end of the day.

Malik: Hey u. I hope you're having a good day. You were on my mind and I just wanted to say hello.

Me: Hello, handsome. My day has been hectic but it's nothing I can't handle. How's your day going?

Malik: I'm working on the twelfth hour. Hopefully, I'll be wrapping things up in a couple hours. This is what I signed up for.

Me: Awwww poor thing. Don't work too hard now. The ladies need the sexy doctor in LA by their side while they heal LOL

Malik: Nah, the women aren't the ones that's been needing my attention. These niggas out here wildin' out. I've had about six gunshot victims today alone. That's not counting the ones I had when I came on last night smh. But I have to get back to work, luv. I'll talk to you once you get home tonight. Be careful out there and keep it tight for me.

Toni didn't bother to reply because Malik nine times out of ten put his phone on do not disturb the moment he pressed send. She would never be able to handle the job he had. The sight of blood turned her stomach. To see it on a regular basis was something she couldn't deal with. And the thought of all the bloodshed going on in the streets of the United States was endless. Wishing she was waiting for Malik at his home after seeing all that, Toni went to her phone and placed an order. She wanted to keep his mental fresh as he dealt with the darkness of the hoodlums that had no kind of guidance out there.

After completing the order that she sent to the hospital where Malik worked, Toni gathered her purse and put her phone inside as she removed her keys. Leaving out of her office, Toni stopped at Jasper's door and leaned on the doorframe as she watched him work diligently on whatever had his undivided attention.

"Aye, I'm out of here for lunch. Do you want me to bring something back?" she asked, causing her boss to raise his head.

"That sounds like a plan. I don't think I will be able to leave out any time soon. Don't rush back. I'll be alright until you return. How's the Dryer affidavit coming along?"

"I working on it, but it's a hot-ass mess. You have your work cut out for you on that one. I'll keep my comments to myself, but you already know what I'm thinking." Toni rolled her eyes before pushing off the door frame. "Good luck with that though."

"I was thinking about that myself, to be honest," Jasper said squeezing the bridge of his nose. "There's not enough money in the world for me to lie for profit and in this case, I will have to do a lot of lying to win this case. I'm going to follow my first mind and back out. Thanks, Antonia. You didn't voice what's on your mind, but trust me, I hear you loud and clear."

Toni tapped the wooded frame and walked away. What's right is right. Jasper would've been the one struggling to live with the fact that the man he was represented swore up and down the allega-tions against him was false. She believed every complaint was true and his nasty ass touched those girls inappropriately.

Toni was still heated when she made it to her car. Pushing the button to bring the engine to life in her 2020 Volkswagen Passat, she turned the air conditioning up to cool off because she was hot under the collar. Jasper was making the right decision because he had daughters of his own. The thought of some perverted bastard touching any child would've automatically made Toni decline the case. Wouldn't have been much she needed to think about to decide either. It would've been on sight, before they were finished explain-ing what happened.

Finding an empty spot in the parking lot of the restaurant ten minutes or so later, Toni snatched up her purse from the floor of the passenger seat and got out of her vehicle. She hit the lock button on her key fob and made her way inside because she needed a drink to calm herself down. Looking around, she didn't see her friends at first, but spotted them in the back of the establishment. Toni hur-riedly made her way in their direction in a haste.

"What the hell is wrong with you?" Baylei asked with a frown.

"Girl, work shit. It's okay because Jasper isn't going to continue the case," Toni stressed as she took a seat. Seeing that one of her girls took the liberty to order a cocktail for her and that lightened her mood a little bit. Toni sucked down the contents in the glass quickly and waved at the waitress to get another one.

"Nah, bitch. It's not okay if you're drinking like that. Talk to us. What's going on?" Jordyn asked.

"You know damn well I can't talk about the cases at my damn job. Just know that I can't stand a pedophile muthafucka. The shit pisses me off to the max. Anyway, let's talk about something else."

The two people that sat at the table with Toni knew she loved her job and if she could've, she would go deeper. So instead of pres-suring her to talk about the dilemma, they left it alone. The waitress came back to their table and Toni put in her drink order as well as what they wanted to eat. Toni also put in Jasper's order, but let the woman know she didn't want it made until she was almost ready to leave.

Baylei smiled down at her phone. She'd never blushed so much when she was with Noah. Chade had her in a place that looked damn good on her. Baylei deserved everything that man brought her way and her friends were standing by her side for it all. Chade proposed fairly quickly, but the two of them were still loving one another from afar. Baylei refused the offer to move to California for the moment because she wanted to make sure all of her ducks were in a row before moving across the country.

"It's been a minute since we've been able to hang out. I have to tell y'all what the fuck Elizabeth's ass had the nerve to do," Baylei said irritably.

The mention of Noah's mama had Toni and Jordyn propped on their elbows waiting for her to spill the tea. When Noah passed away, Baylei didn't shed a tear. What he and Ashley had done was the ultimate betrayal in her eyes. What happened to them was well deserved and she waited for the day to hear the news of their demise.

"Since she found out what her son did, she has been harassing the fuck out of me. I finally stopped taking her for a joke and put a restraining order on her ass," Baylei said taking a sip of her drink.

"What did the son of a bitch do?" Toni asked.

"I'll get to it in a minute. Can I tell you what happened my way, please? Baylei asked, rolling her eyes. When Toni didn't say anything else, she continued.

"Elizabeth had the nerve to come to my house raging like a fuckin' bull last week. When I opened the door, she demanded I give back the money her family worked hard for. Y'all, I stood in my doorway looking at her ass like the crazy woman she appeared to be at the time. That woman called me black everything in any language she could muster up."

"What money is she trying to get back? And why didn't you call me when all this shit took place?" Toni asked with an attitude. "You of all people know I don't discriminate against nobody. I would've beat her old ass on your front porch."

"That's the main reason I didn't tell yo' loony ass about it. Anyway, I found out a little while ago that Noah put me in his will—"

"Shut the front door!" Toni screamed loudly. Baylei shot her an evil eye, causing Toni to snap her lips closed tightly.

"If you would stop interrupting me, maybe I could tell you what the hell happened. And stop making all that damn noise in these people's establishment. Everybody don't need to know my damn business, Toni," Baylei huffed. "Noah at some point put me down as his beneficiary on an insurance policy without informing me. Not to mention, all of his assets were put in my name as well." The shocked expressions on her friends' faces were priceless. "We would've been triplets if we were together that day because that's exactly how I looked hearing the news."

They were laughing when the waitress came over with a cart filled with their food and Toni's drink. Once their orders were placed before them, Toni had more to say.

"Noah did all that bullshit to you and in the end, he was still giving his money to the woman he tried to get rid of. Karma is a bitch, and his mama better watch the fuck out because she's coming for her evil ass next."

"I know that shit right, sis." Jordyn cackled just loud enough not to disturb others. "Noah knew what he was doing, but he didn't get the chance to reverse that shit before he kicked the bucket. What's that saying? You reap what you sow. Yeah, that's what happened to him."

"With the position I'm in right now, the last thing I need is any type of heat coming my way. If it was left up to me, I'd get a certain somebody to make her disappear." Baylei smirked. "Elizabeth better leave me the hell alone while she can. I have enough to worry about without her putting in a helping hand."

"Tell us about this position you're in though. What else have you been mum about with your secretive ass? Life should be great for the future Mrs. Oliver," Jordyn sang with a smile.

"And you bet' not be pregnant either," Toni added.

"Pregnant? Hell, my fiancé wouldn't even know about that one. We not doing that shit right now." Baylei laughed.

"How do you accept a proposal but don't want to have the man's kids? Where the fuck they do that at?"

"Toni, to be honest, Chade jumped the gun asking me to marry him. It's barely been a month since we met in person and that's not nearly enough time to get married. Another thing, he lives in California with no intentions of moving back to Chicago. I have a whole career here and I'm not leaving anytime soon. Anybody that knows me, knows my money is more important than anything and I would never allow a man to take care of me while I find another position in my field."

"Man, listen to your ass. There's no time period that says you have to wait to get married. Baylei, in the short timeframe, that man has proven the love he has for you is real. I think you need to stop playing games because Mr. Lover Man is off the market because of you. He can have any bitch that walks up smiling in his face."

Baylei looked at Toni as if she was going to haul off and knock her head between the booth and the window. All her friend did was hunch her shoulders while drinking from her glass of water.

"Toni has a point, but that's not my business. Tell us about the tea you've been holding back, since you're not pregnant."

Baylei rolled her eyes and put a spoonful of mac and cheese in her mouth. After swallowing, she cleared her throat.

"Let me finish telling y'all the rest of the story first. Obviously, Elizabeth doesn't know about the insurance policy, but she found out about everything else. One thing she said while standing on my porch was, my black ass didn't deserve a dime from her son. I didn't let on that I knew what she was referring to. I just slammed the door in her face."

Jordyn and Toni laughed uncontrollably.

"Man, that was your Karen moment, Lei! You passed that shit up too nicely. Now, if that was me, I would've been stomping her like an Atomic Dog while recording her ass for the internet. That's a charge I would've taken without hesitation.." Toni was a damn fool, but Baylei knew she was serious.

"Elizabeth stayed on the porch beating on my door for well over an hour. My neighbors must've gotten tired of her making all the noise and called the police. When they arrived, Elizabeth lied and said I assaulted her. Do y'all know these muthafuckas took her word over mine and was about to lock my ass up? I continuously told them she was lying, but they weren't listening until I told them I would sue the hell out of the City of Chicago if they touched me."

"What the fuck? How the fuck they were going to arrest you off her word?" Toni asked angrily.

"It was a racial situation that I flipped on their ass. One of the officers grabbed me by the arm and I snatched away. I told his ass that I had surveillance footage that was recording as we spoke. The look in his eyes told how spooked he was at that moment. His partner pulled me to the side and eventually went inside the house with me to view the cameras. When he saw for himself that Elizabeth lied through her teeth, he arrested her for violating the restraining order after I presented that too."

"Good for her ass," Toni clapped. "I still say you should've whooped that trick."

"Nah, I can't stoop to her level. I have too much to lose. I'll tell y'all why. I've inherited a large sum of money."

"What's your definition of a large sum of money?" Jordyn asked.

"I'm only disclosing this to y'all because we're family. I'm worth millions," Baylei whispered.

"Just run your face into my hand real hard so I can slap the shit outta you," Toni sneered. "I don't give a damn how much you're worth. I'm still an average bitch, in the eyes of the public! I could've beat the fuck out of Elizabeth's pale ass!"

"Toni, shut up!" both Baylei and Jordyn said in unison.

They were all quiet for a good minute while they ate their lunch. Toni thought about everything Baylei revealed and chuckled out of the blue. There was so much she wanted to ask, but she didn't want to upset her friend. The day would come when Baylei would tell the entire story when she was ready. She put her foot in her mouth by saying she wasn't leaving her job to be with Chade. Baylei didn't need a job with the money she was blessed with. The way Toni saw it, her friend was scared of change and was prolonging her move for whatever reason.

"Until then, I will be there for all the smoke. 'Cause when you see her, you see me. And I'm with all the shit," Toni said, pointing between herself and Baylei.

Chapter 3

While sitting cross-legged in the lounge chair outside of the home she shared with Malik, Ailani stared blankly at nothing in particular. Her mind had been roaming for the past couple days since she had spoken with Malik. The conversation didn't go as she expected because he'd asked a question Ailani wasn't prepared to answer. After the call ended without warning, Ailani had repeatedly called the man she came to love throughout the years to no avail. Malik refused to talk.

The question of how he knew plagued her mind. Ailani had hidden the relationship with Dexter, better known as Dex, for two years. She'd started seeing him after literally bumping into him at the concession stand at a Dodger's game she and Malik were attending. When Ailani rushed to get something to eat between innings, she had knocked Dex's hotdog from his hand and apologized, immediately offering to buy him another.

Dex wasn't worried about the wiener that he lost. He wanted the beautiful dark-skinned beauty standing before him. Ailani explained that she was involved with someone, but that was the least of Dex's concerns. When he had his eye on something, he usually got what he wanted. That particular day was no different. Ailani smiled at the compliments Dex shot at her and eventually took his number.

With the hours Malik worked at the hospital, Ailani became lonely many days. Spending time with her friends was something she rarely did because in Ailani's mind, they were jealous of her. Having a man of Malik's caliber was difficult when you had friends who were known to fuck any and everything if they could. Malik wasn't going to fall prey to them, and that's why Ailani kept her man away from that circle.

Ailani met Malik when she was discharged from the hospital after being admitted for a mental evaluation. She had been in the psych ward for seven days and was on her best behavior to prove she didn't belong there. As she was leaving, Malik, looking good as hell in his scrubs and lab coat entered the elevator with her. They sparked up a conversation and exchanged numbers. On their first date, Ailani conjured up a story about losing her family in a fire. The empathy in Malik's eyes was so sincere.

From that day forward, Malik texted to ask about her day and even sent flowers to her place of work. Ailani was an assistant at an office building at the time and really wanted to capture the heart of the handsome doctor. She knew if she bagged him, her financial troubles would be history. Ailani was living paycheck to paycheck and could barely make ends meet. But with the help of credit cards, she made it work for herself while digging a hole in her credit.

The closer she and Malik became, the more Ailani did whatever it took to get into his pockets. Cooking, cleaning, fucking and sucking him good, got her into the door of his home after just five months. Malik made sure her bank account, which he opened, stayed in good standings. With a man that was making six figures as a doctor, Ailani didn't think she needed to work another day.

A year into their relationship, she came up with a lie about getting laid off from the company she worked for, stating they were downsizing. Malik tried his best to help Ailani find another job, but she kept saying every company filled the positions she applied for. He provided for her without thought, but the subject always came up. Once Malik started trusting that she wasn't after his money and genuinely showed she loved him, he gave Ailani full control of his finances. Everything was good until a few months prior when Malik came home earlier than expected and got the mail before Ailani could check the box.

Malik blew a gasket when he learned she hadn't paid the mortgage, car note, or any of the other bills. Questioning where his money was going, Ailani blamed it all on shopping when all along, she was splurging on expensive trips and gifts for Dex and herself. Dex wasn't a user by far. He provided for Ailani as well, but she wanted to show him that she also was in the position to take care of her man too.

There were no questions asked when it came to Ailani's and Dex's relationship. They appeared to be a happy couple and spent lots of time together. When Malik was working twelve to forty-eight hours at the hospital, Dex was lying in bed with Ailani or digging out her insides in sexual pleasure. It wasn't often that she would allow him to come over because she didn't want to get caught. Ailani was very careful with how she moved with Dex, so for Malik to ask about him was a shock.

Racking her brain, a light bulb went off in Ailani's head. She remembered the day she saw Selena in the grocery store when Malik and his friends went to Vegas. Ailani got up from the position she was in and paced through the grass.

"Selena, you bitch! Why couldn't you have minded your business?" Ailani screamed. "I know she told Samir and he ran back to his boy like the fucktard he is. This bitch is about to hear from me."

Ailani stormed into the house just as the doorbell rang. She wasn't expecting anyone and the only time someone would ring the doorbell is if she had a delivery. Ailani hadn't ordered anything in a while. As she walked to the door, there was a FEDEX worker on the porch. Thinking nothing of it, Ailani opened the door.

"Good afternoon, ma'am. I have a certified letter for Miss Ailani Denton. Would that be you?" the handsome man asked.

"Yes, that's me."

"Okay. I need you to sign here," he said, pointing to the electronic device he had in hand. When Ailani finished scribbling her John Hancock, he handed her a flat envelope and walked away.

Ailani watched his back flex as he made his way to the truck. Shaking her head with a smile, she turned to go back in the house with a vision of her legs wrapped around his waist dancing in her head. Shaking away the thought, Ailani slowly peeled the envelope open and pulled out the papers inside. Scanning the document quickly, she had to go back and read again; slowly.

"Son of a bitch! How dare he call himself evicting me?"

Ailani continued reading and noticed there were two other attempts to get the documents to her. The dates were from a couple weeks prior to just the week before. Both times she knew exactly where she was, and it wasn't at her home. If she had been there to get the delivery the first time, it would've given Ailani more time to prepare for the eviction. Hell, she probably would've been able to sweet talk her way out of the process. Instead, she had less than fourteen days to find somewhere to lay her head.

Stomping up the stairs to her bedroom, Ailani grabbed her phone and called Dex. She listened to the phone ring several times before his voicemail picked up. As she listened to the message, she thought about any way she could make Malik's life more miserable than he was trying to make hers. At the sound of the beep, Ailani left a message for Dex, making sure she sounded defeated.

"Dex, please call me, baby. I really need to talk to you. It's important." She sniffled a little bit before ending the call.

Ailani sat on the side of her bed with her finger hovering over Malik's name on her phone. She said a silent prayer and tapped the button and activated the speaker. Waiting for Malik to answer the phone, she became frustrated each time the phone rang. When he didn't pick up, she let out a high-pitched scream.

Malik had never ignored her to the magnitude that he had been carrying on as of late. Ailani speculated on the situation for a moment and came to the conclusion of Malik having another woman in his life. To further inspect her suspicions, Ailani went to the T-Mobile website and signed into his account. When she was able to get in, she smiled because while he was trying to leave her alone, he hadn't changed any of his information other than his bank account.

Scrolling down his call log, Ailani noticed a number which appeared frequently starting from about a month prior. She took a screen shot of the number and logged out of the account. Googling the area code, Ailani realized the number was located to an individual in Chicago. Malik didn't know anyone in Chicago outside of Chade's family and there was no way he was talking to a man at one and two in the morning. Being the woman that she was, Ailani went to her photos and dialed the number quickly.

Ailani glanced at the clock and it was a little past one in the afternoon. A soft voice answered the phone and horns rose from the top of her head. Ailani knew the woman on the other end wasn't ready for the filth she was about to present into her life.

"Hello?"

"Um, yeah. I found your number in my husband's phone and I need to know what business do the two of you have to discuss in the wee hours of the morning?" The line became completely quiet and Ailani waited patiently for the call to disconnect. When that didn't happen, she continued to wait for the woman on the other end to reply. "You have nothing to say, huh?"

"Hold on for a minute," she said as a door slammed and the sound of her heels clicking at a fast pace. "If the phone cuts off, I'll call your ass *right* back."

As soon as she uttered those words, Ailani's phone went back to the home screen. She dialed the number back and it went straight to voicemail. Trying two more times with the same results, Ailani tossed the phone on the bed next to her and got up and went to the closet to get an outfit out for the day. As she pulled a white halter top from the hanger, her device rang. Rushing back to the bed, Ailani snatched up the phone and hurriedly answered it after seeing the Chicago number clear as day.

"Hello," she said with attitude.

"Okay, Baby girl. Can you please explain why the fuck you called my phone on this young-ass shit? Whoever the fuck your man is, that's who the hell you need to be checking, not me. See, what you don't want is to be coming at me about ya nigga because you gon' run to the car crying when I give you the business straight with no chaser. As a matter fact, who the fuck is yo' husband?"

The sweet and innocent tone was long gone. The woman on the other end of Ailani's phone was straight hood with it and that took her by surprise. She snapped out of her stupor in time to snap back at the woman.

"Damn, bitch, how many muthafuckas you sleeping with?" Ailani asked, laughing. "So you won't be confused about whom I'm calling about, his name is Malik. Do you know him?"

"The jokes on you and you bet' not use that bitch word too loosely. You already got me acting out of character by engaging in this high school shit, *Ailani*." The woman had Ailani stuck once again when she mentioned her name with pure sarcasm.

"How you know my name?" She asked angrily.

"See, you didn't do your homework before reaching out to *the bitch*. You opened the door for me to read yo' shiesty ass to filth. To answer your question, the business we have at the hours you mentioned is therapeutic for both of us. It's the time he tells me how he wishes he was between my legs sopping up my juices with a biscuit, bitch. I explained you wasn't ready for the tea I had for you, boo. But you pushed a button that set me to go." The woman laughed in Ailani's ear.

"As far as me knowing your name, obviously I learned it from your *husband*. If it makes you feel better, my name is Toni. Store it in your memory bank because you will hear it pretty often. Now back to the subject at hand. You say Malik is your husband, right? Well, I'm here to let you know, he don't refer to you as wifey. If I remember correctly, you're a gold digging, stealing when you didn't have to, conniving, cheating-ass bum that he wants out of his shit. So it's a mystery why you're knocking down my phone talking about a man who gets sick the moment a thought of you enters his mind. I'll wait because I got time today, sis."

"There's no way Malik isn't claiming me as his wife. You said all that you did to try to make me feel bad."

"Nah, wrong again. You made yourself feel bad when you fucked up what you had with that man, and it's okay to cry. Malik is a grown-ass man, and when he let me know you meant nothing to him, that made him single in my eyes. I'm done with this bullshit right here. Don't ever call my phone again because I don't have anything to do with the relationship you have with Mr. Daniels. I can only vouch for what I have going on with Malik. I want you to enjoy the rest of your day and keep your head up."

Toni hung up before Ailani could respond and that made her madder than reading the eviction notice that came in the mail. Malik had some explaining to do about his little girlfriend in Chicago and why she had a damn eviction notice to get out of the house they shared together. He was going to tell her what she wanted to know.

Chapter 4

"See you Saturday, Dr. Daniels," one of the nurse assistants sang as Malik walked past to leave for the night.

Waving his hand over his head without turning around, Malik kept walking to the elevator. He was very strict with the policy he put in place for himself; never mix business with pleasure. The women at Cedars Sinai were looking for a meal ticket and Malik learned his lesson with that the hard way with Ailani. The only reason Toni even had a chance with him was because she made her own money.

Stepping off the elevator into the garage, Malik made his way to his car and hit the locks when he got closer. As he sat in the seat and put on his seatbelt, his phone rang and he started the engine before answering. The call automatically connected to the Bluetooth.

"What's up, Big Booty Judy?"

"Malik, don't play with me," Toni laughed. "I hope you're not busy. I have something I want to talk to you about."

"Holla at me."

"I received a call today and I would like to know how Ailani got my number?"

Malik had put the gear in drive but instantly threw it back in park after hearing what Toni said. He just knew he heard her wrong and thought she said Ailani called her. Knowing he hadn't been around that woman in damn near a month, her getting ahold of Toni's number was impossible.

"Come again?"

"How did your wife, get my number, Malik?"

"Hold up, I don't have a wife. If I heard you correctly, you said Ailani called you. Am I correct?" Malik asked.

"Yes, she called asking what our late-night calls were about? How do she know we're communicating, let alone at what time?" Toni asked quizzingly. "Don't get it twisted, I'm not jealous by any means. I just need to know, if you're still involved with this woman, why are you trying to pursue anything me?"

Malik understood exactly where Toni was coming from and she had every right to feel the way she was feeling. Ailani crossed the line contacting her and she was going to hear from him about the bullshit she was destined to stir up. With Ailani contacting Toni, that put doubt in her mind and made Malik look like a liar that wanted to have his cake and eat it too. Which was far from the case. What he had with Toni was real and there was nothing going to get in the way of that; damn sure not Ailani.

"I'm not involved with her at all. I have talked to her since I've been back in L.A., but that didn't go too well because she became an instant mute. As far as her being my wife, that's a whole lie and a half. We weren't ever married. The only reason Ailani was around long as she was is because she doesn't have any family and I felt sorry for her ass. But once she stepped out of line and contacted you, she fucked up royally. The only way I can think of her getting your number is through my account. I'm going to change that password soon as I get off the phone with you."

Toni was quiet for a spell but that didn't last too long. "Well, she will think twice about calling me again because I gave her ass an earful. Malik, I try to stay away from drama because of my profession, but I want you to know, I can be the wrong one to step to and my inner ghetto emerges instantaneously. The only reason she was safe from these hands is because she's all the way in Cali. Handle that bitch before I put in a personal day to fly out and fuck her up."

Malik laughed because he knew how serious Toni was about beating Ailani's ass. Before he could respond, another call came through from his mother. "Aye, let me hit you back. My ma is calling."

"Okay. I'll talk to you later."

Switching over, Malik could hear ruckus in the background and the hairs rose on the back of his neck. His mother was cussing like a sailor while his father tried to calm her down by telling her to go into the house. Of course, Cookie; what everyone called her, wasn't trying to hear any of that.

"Little girl, I'd advise you to get in your car and away from my damn house. Malik don't want you!"

"Cookie, you're the reason he's so soft. You need to take the titty out his mouth so he can be a man! Long as u keep coddling him, he's gonna continue to play with folks' feelings. Y'all should've taught him that playing with a woman can get his ass hurt badly."

Ailani talking crazy to his mama sent Malik into a rage. He jerked the gear into to drive and headed in the direction of his parent's home. Traffic was going to be a bitch and Malik was ready to tackle the commute. Continuing to listen to the back and forth bickering between the ladies, Malik finally decided to at least try to see if his mother would acknowledge him on the phone.

"Ma, stop arguing with that damn girl!" he screamed. "Ma! Ma!"

"Malik, you better talk to this hussy before I put my foot in her ass!" His mama scowled.

"Ohhhh, you got your punk-ass son on the phone and he can't seem to pick up the phone when I call. How sway." Ailani laughed. "Malik, bring yo' ass on because I will be here terrorizing your parents until you talk to me!"

"Nah, you gon' be sprawled out on the front lawn when he pulls up because you're about to be unconscious from the blow I deliver to your disrespectful ass."

"Ma, go in the house and let her talk to herself. I'm on my way. I'll see you in a minute."

Malik drove over the speed limit, dodging in and out of cars to get to his mama faster. He could still hear his mama going in on Ailani and he didn't like that shit one bit. She could be mad at him all day if that's what she wanted to do, but the disrespect toward his mother was a no go. Ailani better hope she thought about her actions and was gone by the time he pulled into the driveway.

It took him an additional twenty minutes to make it to his parents' house and the police were already there trying to defuse the situation. From the looks of things, Ailani was on the verge of going to jail. She was acting a plumb fool with the police and kept saying she wasn't leaving until she was able to talk to Malik.

As Malik exited his car, an officer walked in his direction, intercepting his approach to the scene. "Are you Malik Daniels?" he asked, standing in front of Malik.

"Yes, I am. Would y'all get her off my parents' property? I have nothing to say to that woman today or any other day, for that matter."

"Fill me in on the problem between you all, please."

"There isn't a problem on my part. I ended the relationship and she don't want to let go, I guess," Malik explained, crossing his arms over is chest.

"You ain't ended shit, Malik! Why is this the first of me hearing this bullshit? I've been calling you and haven't talked to you yet! If you don't want me, tell me that shit right now, motherfucker!" Ailani was trying to come over to where Malik was standing, but the other officer kept pushing her back. "I got a certified letter of eviction. Really, Malik? Where the fuck am I supposed to go?" she cried.

"Don't say anything to her. Have you seen Miss Denton prior today?"

"Nope. I talked to her a couple days ago, but she refused to answer a question I'd asked and I hung up. She's been calling since, but I haven't answered any of her calls. To be honest, I just want her out of my crib so I can sell that muthafucka. After that, we have nothing else to discuss. She can go her way and I'll continue doing what I've been doing."

Malik glared in Ailani's direction and the tears that flowed down her face didn't faze him at all. Usually when she cried it would pull at his heartstrings. Now he wished she would drown in them. The taste of bile was heavy in his mouth, causing him to turn his head and spit on the grass. Ailani was acting out in a way Malik never witnessed and he wanted to make sure he was covered before she went ballistic.

"I would like to file a restraining order because I have a feeling this isn't going to be the end of the madness. She has to leave my home and I believe she's going to try to damage my property," Malik said lowly.

"I don't think we need to go far as that, Mr. Daniels—"

His response was interrupted by Ailani's outburst. "You want me out of your house, Malik? You gon' have to come put me out of that bitch! I'm going to tear that muthafucka up so bad you won't be able to give it away. If you wanted to be with someone else, that's all you had to say in the first place. You didn't have to go behind my back!"

"You mean the way you've been fucking around behind my back, Ailani? Come on, man. You're mad you got caught and I'm not about to sit back and be the sucka-ass nigga you thought I was. The things I did for you was because of the love I had for your slick ass! Why the fuck were you with me, huh? For my fuckin' money, bitch!"

"Stop talking to her, Sir!" the officer said, standing directly in front of Malik, blocking his view.

"Lock his ass up! He's a drug dealer and I have proof in our home. Nigga, I told you to stop playing with me. I've kept all of your secrets far too long. You don't want me, then you gon' serve your time in jail!"

Malik laughed because Ailani was doing the most. If there were drugs in that house, he had nothing to do with that shit. She'd set herself up for failure because he wasn't going down for whatever she was into. His paper trail was solid and he had nothing to worry about. The way the officer's eyebrow rose let me know the wheels were running in his head and he was ready to arrest everybody on the scene.

"Is what she is saying true?"

Motioning toward the scrubs he wore, Malik smirked. "Hell nawl! If there's drugs in that house, that's all on her ass. I've been out of the house for damn near a month and just returned to California a week ago. I make over a hundred grand but I'm a fuckin' doctor and I have tax documents for every dime I've earned. I don't have much money anymore because that bitch sucked me dry. You have my permission to go in and search. You don't need a warrant either. As a matter of fact, I'll ride over there with you."

Malik was seeing red after Ailani tried to throw him to the wolves off a lie that spewed from her lips. She stood smirking but little did she know, the joke was about to be on her ass. The officer was on the phone trying to get the ball rolling to get his hands on the drugs she claimed were in the damn house. Malik would have to go gather every receipt he had to clear his name along with proof that he didn't reside at the residence. Malik didn't have cameras inside, but there were plenty on the outside, and that alone would prove he hadn't stepped foot on the property in a month.

It took three hours for the officers to get a warrant and both Malik and Ailani was detained so no one could try to get rid of the evidence. Being booked in a jail cell was the last thing Malik thought would occur that day. He took the time to think about all the things he sacrificed for Ailani to be slapped in the face with her betrayal and dishonesty. To see the hurt on his parents' faces when he was cuffed and put in the back of the squad car would forever be etched in his mind. Malik knew he'd done nothing wrong and waited out his time in the pissy six by eight cell without worry.

In the end, Malik was let go and Ailani was book on possession with the intent of distributing narcotics. Come to find out, there were two bricks of cocaine in the house and Ailani was blaming all of it on Malik. While he was in the cell, he told one of the officers that was working the case where the surveillance equipment was and where the key to the lock box was located. When they finished the examination, they released him on his own recognizance.

Malik Sr. used that time to change the locks and packed up all of Ailani's things and put them in storage. That was the last straw because his son worked hard to get where he was in life and a woman that didn't want to let go wasn't going to bring him down. There were plenty of black men that didn't want anything for themselves. Malik didn't fit into that category. Any way he could, he was going to be there for his son long as he was doing right.

Standing outside of the precinct, he waited for his one and only child to walk out of the doors. It took an additional thirty minutes before he finally got the opportunity to wrap his arms around Malik and that shit felt good as hell. Malik Sr. was glad his son opened up about what he was going through because if he hadn't, Malik would be serving double digits off the strength of the shit Ailani was doing.

"You alright, son?"

"Not really. I can't believe Ailani tried to set me up being spiteful." Malik shook his head, stepping back from his father.

"Officer Moore stated they have another suspect they are looking into. He's been in the house on many occasions with Ailani. There's footage of him bringing a bag in with him but leaving out empty handed. She was using the house to hold his drugs and they were involved."

"I don't give a damn about any of that shit, Pop. All I want is for her ass to leave me the fuck alone. I want nothing else to do with her snake ass. Take me to get my car s so I can get some sleep. I've been awake since last night and I'm tired. I'll come to the house tomorrow. We can talk more then."

Malik thought about everything that went on as his father led the way to his truck. He couldn't believe Ailani went through the extreme to ruin his life. She didn't succeed so that was a plus, but the shit didn't hurt any less. Someone he loved did that shit to him and her actions made Malik look at trusting a muthafucka differently.

Meesha

Chapter 5

Malik hadn't called nor texted since he ended the call with Toni when his mother called. She didn't sweat it and just went about her way, deciding to pay her aunt Brenda and uncle Rob a visit when she got off work. It had been weeks since she'd seen them. When Toni returned from St. Thomas she was laid up with Malik when she wasn't working and hadn't found the time to pop up. As she rolled slowly down their street, there were kids getting wet under the fire hydrant. Those were the days back in the day and it was good to see kids out enjoying being outside. The sight was one that wasn't seen nowadays, but those were the good days Toni remembered from her childhood.

Even though it was a privilege that her parents were able to move out of the hood when she was younger, her aunt and uncle weren't as fortunate. When Toni's parents died, she hit them with a large sum of money from the insurance and they still refused to leave the home they resided in. Toni didn't care what they did with the money. She was appreciative for them being there to hold her up after losing the two people that meant the most to her. Without Aunt Brenda, which was her mama's sister, and her husband, Toni didn't know where she'd be in life.

Their deaths paralyzed her to the core and she didn't want to get out of the bed some days. Her cousin Tangie was there every step of the way, giving Toni the motivation to get up every day instead of wallowing in the grief that was just about smothering her from the world. The death of her parents was hard on Tangie as well, but she always stayed strong for Toni and dealt with the loss in her own way. While she appeared to be okay, she wasn't.

Tangie was out in the streets of Chicago for years suppressing the loss with the evils of drugs. While she appeared to look okay on the outside, she was hurting so much more on the inside. Toni's mom and dad were more like her parents than Brenda and Rob. Tangie was always at Toni's home and when Sam and Lynchelle were taken away from them, she jumped headfirst into the streets.

The crowd she ran with was foreign to the family and they couldn't keep up with her comings and goings. All they could do was hope and pray she would call with her infamous, "What's up, Cuz? I just called to say I love you." There wasn't a week that went by when Toni didn't hear Tangie's voice or receive a text from her cousin. On the outside looking in, nobody would ever be able to say, "What's going on with Tangie?" She always kept herself up and never seemed off to the outside world. But her family knew something wasn't right. The only thing they could do was make sure she was okay and keep their eyes on her as best as they could.

When Toni parked along the curb in front of her aunt's house, she knew without hearing that Tangie had been into some more shit. Jumping out of the car, she hurried to the porch, where Tangie was talking calmly while her mother yelled at the top of her lungs with tears running down her face.

"You need to stop whatever you're doing! Come in here and lay down for a while, Tangie."

"I'm straight, Ma. Ain't nothing going on with me. I'm just tired from being up for two days."

Toni walked up and Tangie looked over her shoulder to see who was coming up behind her. Toni knew right away that her cousin was higher than a kite. The sight before her caved her heart in. Seeing her fam in that state almost always brought Toni to tears, but she held that shit in because she didn't want to show her hand at the moment. It always came out when she was no longer in the presence of Tangie. It seemed that day wasn't going to be any different. All Toni wanted to do was get her away from the emotions her aunt had on full display.

"Aye, Tangie. Come ride with me," Toni said, walking up the steps.

"I need to make a run first, Cuz. I'll—"

"Aht aht, I'm not trying to hear that shit," she said, grabbing Tangie's arm. "Auntie, we'll be back."

Toni led the way to her car and her cousin followed slowly. They had many talks like the one they would have once both of them were in the car. None of the words ever reached Tangie's mental obviously, because she was still out doing the same shit.

Toni sat waiting for Tangie to get in and let the window down when she saw her pull a cigarette from her pocket. Not being a smoker, Toni allowed her cousin to smoke in her presence if that's what she chose to do. Once Tangie was seated in the passenger seat, Toni waited for her to flame up before she started talking.

"What's going on, Tang? You good?"

"Yeah, Cuz. Everything's good," she said taking a deep pull on the cigarette. "You got a couple dollars I can borrow? I'll give it back on Friday."

"Tangie, you know I'm not putting no cash money in your hand. If you're hungry, I'll take you to get something to eat, but I'm not giving you any money. One thing I'm not going to do is support your habit. I love you, cousin, and I don't want you out here like this. When is enough going to be enough?" Toni asked with tears in her eyes.

"Come on Toni. I'm not doing nothing but popping a pill here and there to keep my mind off shit. We've talked about this before. Everybody grieves differently and this is my way. I'm a'ight, okay?"

"That's the thing. You're not, Tangie. We both know you're not okay and drugs isn't a way to cope with nothing. The pills you're ingesting is bringing you down. You may stop feeling the pain for a few, but reality will always be there when you come down from the high you're using to run from something you can't change the outcome of. Regardless, my mama and daddy are still going to be gone."

"This shit is hitting me harder than a ton of bricks. Sam and Chelle were my parents too!" Tangie cried. "They died and a part of me died right along wit 'em. Toni the drugs take me away from this dark-ass world. I know what I'm doing, Cuz, and I promise, I'm good."

Wiping the tears from her eyes, Tangie licked her lips and stared out of the side window. She laughed lowly and Toni had no choice but to laugh right along with her. Tangie's laugh was one she would always look forward to hearing. Toni reached over and joined hands with her cousin.

"I'll help you beat this shit, Tangie. You just have to want the help. It's been years and it's about time to put this part of your life behind you. There's so much more for you to do than walking around doing drugs."

The sincerity in Toni's voice touched Tangie, but in an instant, she was back to the survivor of the streets she was accustomed to being. "I don't need help, Toni. I got this shit covered. Trust me."

"Okay, I'm going to leave it alone for now. Come inside, eat, and get some sleep. After that, I will take you wherever you want to go. How about that?"

"Bet. I can do that," Tangie agreed, getting out of the car.

When they entered the house, Brenda walked out of the kitchen and smiled. She had fixed both Toni and Tangie a plate of greens, sweet potatoes, cornbread, and fried chicken. The two cousins laughed, smiled, and talked about the things they did back in the day. Reminiscing had them making plans to get together with their other cousins and friends they hadn't seen in a while. Toni filled her in on her trip to St. Thomas and Baylei's engagement. Toni even called Baylei and Jordyn so they could talk to Tangie too. Seeing her truly enjoy the time they were spending together was everything to Toni.

About two hours later, Toni and Tangie went into the bedroom they basically grew up in together and fell asleep with their bellies full. Toni didn't realize how long she'd been asleep until she heard her phone ringing. Sitting up, she reached over and grabbed her phone from her purse and saw it was Malik.

"Hey you," she said with a wide grin on her face. That smile faded away when she looked over and noticed the other side of the bed was empty. Tangie was no longer in the bed and Toni knew she was back in the streets doing what would make her feel better for the moment.

"Did you hear what I said?" Malik asked.

"No, I'm sorry. Would you repeat it?"

"I asked, what you doing?"

"Just waking up at my aunt's house. Let me call you right back, Malik. I have to find out something. I'll call you in a few minutes."

Toni ended the call and put her shoes on before walking out of the room. She found both Brenda and Rob in the living room watching the news. It was well after nine o'clock at night and Toni hadn't planned to sleep so long. As she looked in the kitchen, the bathroom, and the garage, Toni went back into the living room and Brenda answered the question she was thinking without being asked.

"She left about an hour ago. Tangie is going to do what she wants, Toni. We just have to pray because there's nothing we can do about her condition, baby. Tangie is sick and she has to want to get better. Other than that, there's nothing else we can do."

Toni wasn't trying to hear what her aunt said. She was going to get through to her cousin. It had been four years since she started using and Toni knew when it started. The thing was, she didn't know when it was going to end. She was going to continue to keep trying to get Tangie to see that she needed help. Toni wasn't going to give up on her and she would keep loving her as she had been doing all their lives. Regardless of what Tangie was going through, she would always be Toni's little cousin/sister.

Bending over her aunt, Toni hugged her tightly and let it linger a little longer than usual. She walked over to Rob and kissed his cheek before bidding her goodbyes. It took everything in Toni not to go driving around to find her cousin. Instead, she called her phone and listened as it rang until the voicemail picked up.

"Tangie, I want you to be careful out there. Call me when you get a moment. I love you, Cuz."

***

Toni called Malik the minute she got in the car and her emotions were all over the place. She couldn't talk for the first five minutes the call connected. Malik sat and listened to Toni cry as she struggled to see through the fuzziness of her tears. Tangie left Toni in that state every time she chose the streets over reasoning. Even though Toni knew her cousin would call or pop up within the next couple of days, it still didn't matter because of the way she down-played her addiction.

"Are you okay, baby?"

"No, I'm so worried about my cousin. There has to be something I can do to help her," Toni cried, wiping her eyes.

Feeling the need to tell someone outside of family what was going on, Toni opened up to Malik. He listened without interruption and felt all of Toni's pain. With every sniffle, scream, and concern, Toni had every right to feel the way she was at the moment. Malik was formulating a positive way to console her once she finished her rant. He had actually called her to talk about the events of his day, but that would definitely have to wait. Once Toni quieted down, Malik cleared his voice.

"Antonia, I want you to hear me out. I'm sorry you, your cousin, hell, your family, are going through this," Malik started off by say-ing. "I know firsthand what you're going through and it's hard for anyone to deal with. Addiction is an illness. When a person is doing drugs, there's nothing another person can say or do to make them get help. They have to want that help on their own. I know it hurts to see your cousin in that state, but trust me, there's nothing you can do to make them change." Malik paused to allow Toni to say some-thing, but when she didn't, he continued.

"The more you or anyone else push your cousin toward help, the further she's going to travel in the opposite direction. When you talk about her addiction, she hears you, Toni. She's just not ready. All you can do is be there for her and keep letting her know that she's loved. One day she will get tired of doing the same thing and will eventually accept the offer of help you present to her."

"I'm going to find a treatment center and pay for her help, Ma-lik. Tangie needs an intervention and I'm going to set that up for her. I have to," Toni cried.

"And believe me, baby, when you force your hand, she's going to go. But what I want you to understand is this, Tangie is an adult. There's no facility that can hold one against their will. If she's not ready, she will sign herself out of that treatment center and walk the fuck out. Then she will be right back on the streets with the sense of resentment from the ones that cares about her most; her family. Tangie is going to feel like y'all are the ones that's against her when all you were trying to do was help. But in her mind, y'all deceived her. That's not what you want to do. The last thing you want is for her to get lost in these streets. At least now, she's coming around for y'all to see that she's alright."

What Malik said made sense, but Toni wasn't going to sit back and watch her cousin continue to lose herself. She felt as if the world was weighing down on her shoulders and she didn't mind as long as she was able to save her cousin. Toni pulled into her driveway and gathered her purse after cutting off the car. Slowly walking up the steps, she unlocked the door and made her way to the bedroom. All she wanted to do was lay down and sleep.

"Thank you for listening to me, Malik. I'm angry because I don't know what to do. This is too much," she said, shaking her head.

"You don't have to thank me. I'm here whenever you need me. Remember what I said. Tangie has to be the one to determine when she's ready. You can't beat yourself up about this."

"I hear you, Malik. It's going to be hard to see things the way you explained. I won't give up though."

"I'm not saying give up. But prepare yourself for whatever may happen. Good or bad, you have to prepare. Get some sleep and clear your mind. I'm off for the next couple days. We'll catch up tomorrow, okay?"

"Okay. Talk to you later."

Toni ended the call and removed her clothes slowly. Tears stung the back of her eyes and before she knew it, she was on her knees crying to the man above to guide her cousin through this thing called life.

Meesha

Chapter 6

Malik tossed and turned majority of the night thinking about all that
transpired the day before. He woke up with a hard-on that was
bound to put a hole in his sheets if he hadn't got up when he did to
drain the weasel. After taking care of his hygiene, Malik dressed
and was out of his house a little after ten in the morning. The first
stop on his things to-do list was his parent's house. He wanted to
clear the air about the things that were said in the wake of Ailani's
bull crap.

As Malik drove on the highway, the sounds of the Lox "Fuck
You" bumped through the speakers. It'd been a long time since his
blood boiled the way it was at that precise moment. To have the
feelings of murder itching to come out was horrible because the cul-
prit was a female. If Ailani was within his reach, Malik could guar-
antee he would've slapped the taste out of her mouth, going against
everything his mama taught him about putting his hands on a
woman.

Even though Ailani would be sitting in jail for a good minute,
Malik still wanted to shake her ass up for trying to destroy his career
and his livelihood. He hit the R&B station on Sirius XM. He didn't
want his mind to go further into goon mode before he made it to his
destination.

Malik's phone rang and there was an unknown number on the
screen and he declined the call. Whoever it was needed to leave a
message, otherwise they would never reach him.

Getting off at his exit, Malik's stomach growled and he hoped
like hell his mama had cooked breakfast. Turning onto the street his
parents resided, he parked his car in the driveway and cut the engine. Malik grabbed his phone and there was a voicemail waiting
for him to listen to it. Curiosity got the best of him as he hit the play
button and put the phone on speaker.

*"Hello, I'm looking for Malik. This is Alauna, Ailani's mom. I
got your number from her phone and I would like to speak to you*

about whatever transpired between you and my daughter. When-ever you can, please give me a call at (707) 555-0024. I hope to hear from you soon.

Malik sat back in a daze because as far as he knew, Ailani's mama was dead and she never knew who her father was. He had taken her in under false pretenses and the plot had thickened. Ailani was full of lies and the skeletons were falling out of her closet slowly but surely. Malik had no plans of calling the mystery woman back anytime soon, but he knew she would be reaching out to him again.

As he climbed out of his car, his mother appeared on the porch with a slight smile on her face.

"You been out here a little too long. I had to come out and make sure my baby was alright. Bring yo' ass on in here so you can eat. Knowing you, that's why you're at my damn house so early," She laughed.

"Good morning, Ma. I'm doing more than fine, thank you. And for your information, I came through with an empty stomach in tow to smash all the good food I knew you would have in there for me." Cookie smacked her lips with her hands on her hips. "Don't be like that. You spoiled me my whole life. You gotta keep that same energy, woman."

It was Malik's turned to laugh as he climbed the steps walking into his mother's awaiting arms. Malik stepped out of her embrace and opened the door so his mother could enter ahead of him.

"My energy is wearing thin. It's about time for you to get a woman that appreciates the man you are, Lik," Cookie said, calling him by the childhood nickname she gave him. "That damn Ailani wasn't it, and I told you that from the beginning. I kept my mouth closed because I was never the one to get in your business, but the shit she pulled yesterday was ridiculous. Not to mention how she handled your finances. Don't ever give a woman that much control again."

"I know, Ma, and that chapter of my life been over. Ailani lied about too many things and I would never be able to forgive her for any of it. I received a call while I was in the driveway and a lady left a message saying she was Ailani's mama."

"Her mama? That child told me her mother died." Cookie looked at her son with a shocked expressing on her face. "Where the hell has she been all these years?"

"I don't know where she's been, but Ailani had me thinking the same thing from day one. She must've used her phone call to call her mother because the woman said she got my number from Ailani's phone. I'm not calling her back. Excuse my language, but fuck Ailani. She can rot in that jail cell for all I care."

Malik was mad and didn't want to think about Ailani for another moment. Whatever happened to her, she deserved everything the law threw at her. He never thought he would get involved with a woman that took his kindness for weakness, but here he was dealing with a bunch of bullshit with a woman he gave nothing but love.

"I think you should call her back. She probably has something to tell that you know nothing about. If you're going to leave this shit with Ailani in the past, you should close all the doors and throw away the key. There's something wrong with that woman, if you ask me. Who the hell tells the police about drugs and try to pin it on someone else? Didn't she know about the cameras you had installed?"

"Yeah, she knew. Ailani wasn't thinking clearly when she opened her mouth about those drugs. The only thing on her mind was hurting me, and she failed miserably."

"She sure as hell did because now, she's going down for something that nigga got her wrapped up in," Malik Sr. said, walking into the room. "In order for her to get out of this jam, she has to give up the name of the guy that stashed the drugs."

Malik's father walked up to his son and gave him a half hug before sitting at the dining room table. Malik sat across from him while his mother fixed plates in the kitchen. The smell of bacon was pungent in the air along with smothered potatoes with onions, eggs, grits, and toast. When his plate was placed in front of him, Malik wasted no time digging in.

"Son, how long has Ailani been dealing with this dude? Have you ever seen him before?" his father asked.

"It was brought to my attention by Samir while we were in Vegas. Selena saw Ailani with the nigga at the grocery store. If I'd seen them, we wouldn't be going through all this today. Not knowing is bad on my part. Knowing Ailani, her ass pillow talked and the nigga probably knows everything about me, while I'm sitting in the dark trying to figure out who he is."

Cookie joined them at the table and they ate in silence for a few minutes. Malik Sr. sipped from his coffee mug and placed it back onto the table. "I called in a favor at the courthouse and the eviction is in full effect. When you're ready to move everything out, let me know and I'll help," he said, getting up from his seat. Walking into his office, Malik Sr. came out just as fast as he went in with an envelope in hand.

"This was something I've had in place since you were an infant. I wanted to make sure you grew up to be a man with purpose and you have shown me that you are that and more. Me and your mom are proud of the man you have grown to be and with your finances being the way they are, waiting until you're thirty-five doesn't stand anymore."

Malik was confused by his father's words, and the smile on his mother's face only heightened his curiosity. The way his father looked at the envelope let him know whatever was inside was important. Waiting patiently for whatever his father was trying to reveal, Malik continued to eat his breakfast. Clearing his throat, Malik Sr. looked up with tears in his eyes.

"Malik, I want you to take this and do whatever you want to do with it. The only thing I ask is for you to be responsible and plan your future. Oh, and there's no more where this came from, so don't come back to me with your hand held out." Cookie laughed as her husband slid the envelope towards his son.

Ripping opened the envelope, Malik reached inside and read the contents of the letter inside. As he read, his eyes bulged and tears fell on the paper Inside was a letter from Chase Bank informing him of a trust fund his father had set up for him. According to the letter, the trust had been available to him since his twenty-fifth birthday in the amount of a million dollars.

Malik worked hard at his schooling because he wanted to take care of his parents the way they had taken care of him growing up. Whenever he would try to give them money, both of them always turned down his offers. It never occurred to him why until that moment. They didn't need it. His parents never struggled, but Malik didn't know they had it like that. He always assumed they took out loans to put him through school and wanted to pay the money back.

"Don't ask any questions; it's yours. I want you to get a financial advisor and do right by that money, Malik. Not a girlfriend either."

"I don't know what to say. Are you sure you won't go into debt giving me this?" he asked seriously.

"I'm sure." His father laughed.

Malik Sr. wasn't always the laid-back retired truck driver. In his prime, he was a big-time drug dealer that ran the mean streets of Detroit, Michigan. When Cookie revealed she was pregnant, Malik Sr. got to work to get her away from his dealings in the street. He didn't want his child raised in the environment of the inner city. Within months of getting the news, he moved Cookie to the suburbs of California. Two years later, he was out of the game for good and was sitting on enough money to never have to work another day of his life.

He raised his only child, his son, to work hard for everything in life and it paid off. He never wanted Malik to run to the streets to get rich quickly. The last thing Malik Sr. wanted was his son getting killed trying to hustle. When Malik became a doctor, his parents were proud and knew he was on his way. Ailani set him back when she mismanaged his funds, but as long as Malik Sr. had breath in his body, his son was going to always be alright.

Malik was in a daze as he read the letter again. He stood and kissed his mother. His father rose to his feet as his son walked around the table and hugged him for dear life. Tears soaking through the shoulder of his father's shirt, Malik pounded his hand on his dads back repeatedly. The fifty thousand he won in Vegas wasn't shit compared to the gift he was given.

"Thank you for always being there for me. You have been there every step of the way and I promise not to let you down again," Malik said, stepping out of the embrace.

"You didn't let me down. As I said before, we're all blinded at some time of our lives. I've been there too. Long as you learn from the mishap and don't get distracted, you will be alright. This shit with Ailani was a lesson. The right woman will come into your life sooner than later, and she's going to do right by you. Just make sure she's not the type that needs all the time. The woman you want should be able to do as much for you as you do for her."

His father's words took Malik's mind right to Toni and he smiled. Time would tell how far their relationship would go. To be honest, Toni was his woman, but Malik didn't want to speak on it prematurely.

"I met someone, but we're taking things slow. I actually met her in St. Thomas while at Ahmad's wedding. She is the woman Ailani spoke of yesterday. She called that woman and got her feelings hurt. It was part of the reason she went as far as she did in front of the house," Malik explained.

"Good for her ass. Maybe that would teach her to stop looking for shit because she shole did find it. Ailani is lucky that woman didn't find her and whoop her tail," Cookie said, rising to clear the table.

"If Toni didn't live in Chicago, I'm quite sure she would've. That's one feisty woman."

"Tell me a little bit about this woman, son," his father said.

"Her name is Toni. She's a thirty-two-year-old paralegal, no children, and from Chicago." Malik's cheeks got hot thinking about the woman he was falling head over hills for. If he wasn't so dark, his father would be able to see him blushing like a damn girl.

"Now, that's a grown-ass woman with a good head on her shoulders. Those Chitown women don't play son."

"How the hell you know, Malik? Make me beat your ass. In there talking about another damn woman. You must be outta your mind," Cookie yelled from the kitchen.

"See what I mean? She ain't even from Chicago, but Detroit ain't too far away. One of the same," he said, shaking his head. "Ain't nobody talking about no damn woman. I'm telling my son about the woman he's pursuing. I told him to be careful before he finds a woman like his gangsta-ass mama." Malik and his father shared a laugh waiting for Cookie to emerge from the kitchen.

"I doubt if he finds anyone like me. I'm custom made and there isn't another out there like me. Your bighead ass knows this already. Keep playing and you will be on the next episode of *The First 48.*"

"That's my cue to get out of here. I'm not about to be a witness to none of that. I may have to put my skills to work on my day off and I don't work for free," Malik laughed at his own joke. "A'ight, Pops. Thanks again and I'll get up with you soon. I'm about to go pop up on Chade. It's Thursday and you know that's guys' night out. Since I'm off, I just want to talk to him before we get with the guys."

"You don't have to explain anything to me. Be careful out there though. I love you, son."

"I love you too." Malik moved to the kitchen to love on his mother. "I'm out of here, old lady—"

"What I tell you about calling me that shit? Always trying to blow up my spot."

"Ma, you older than me, so you're an old lady." Cookie threw a dishrag at Malik and he ducked just in time. "I love you, Mama," he said kissing her cheek.

"I love you too, baby. And call that woman to see what the hell she has to say. I want to hear all about it too because I know that crazy-ass girl hiding a lot of shit."

Malik agreed to make the call and promised he would tell his mama all about it. The only thing about his agreement was that he didn't say *when* he would do it.

Leaving his parents' home, Malik climbed into his ride and thought about calling Chade to let him know he was coming to his job, but decided to sneak up on him instead.

***

Malik went to the bank after leaving his parents and was beaming from ear to ear. The process went smoothly and he opened another account with business ventures swarming in his head. Driving through the California traffic, Toni crossed his mind. It was after noon and he hadn't attempted to hit her up.

"Hey, Siri, call Toni," he said loudly.

"Calling Toni," the automated voice said in the chipper voice that irritated the hell out of Malik. The phone rang until it went to voicemail.

He waited until he was summoned to leave a message but was greeted with the "This message box is full", which puzzled Malik. Toni was in a fucked-up head space the night before, but why wouldn't she answer any of her calls? With her being in Chicago, there was nothing he could do except wait it out.

Pulling in the parking lot of Chade's place of employment, Malik slid in the space right next to his homie's Camaro and got out. Joseline sat up in her chair soon as he walked through the door. Every time he visited, the Latina mamí always fucked him with her eyes while licking her lips seductively.

"It's good to see you, Malik. How you been?" Joseline asked, batting her eyes.

"I'm good. Chade busy right now?"

"No, I don't think so, but I'll let him know you're here." Joseline stood up, poking her ass out as she retrieved the phone on her desk. Malik didn't know why she was doing all the extra because he wasn't studying her like that. All he wanted to do was chop the shit with his boy. She could keep the rest of that shit.

"You can go back. Mr. Oliver is waiting for you."

Nodding his head at her, Malik made his way to Chade's office. Joseline took the opportunity to talk her shit as he walked down the hall. "I'm going to get the chance to taste all that chocolate one of these. Damn, that nigga fine!" Joseline was thirstier than the Sahara Desert with the way she threw herself at Malik. She was the reason he tried his best not to visit Chade at work.

Chade was concentrating on the computer screen with precision when Malik sat down in front of his desk. As he waited, his phone chimed with a text, prompting Malik to see what was up. When he saw a number that wasn't saved in his phone appear, he opened the message quickly.

(707) 555-0024: Malik, this is Alauna again. I left you a voicemail and I have yet to hear from you. I don't know if you are aware, Ailani is in jail and I really need to talk to you.

Malik's eyebrows furrowed and he was irritated because Alauna should've been hounding the nigga Ailani's ass had been spending all her time with. There was no way he was doing anything to help her out of the jam she created on her own. His first thought was to block her, but he changed his mind because eventually, she would come out and say what she actually wanted to discuss. Until then, fuck both of them.

"What got you over there about to bust a blood vessel?" Chade asked, rolling his sleeve up past his elbow.

"Man, Ailani's fuckin' mama!"

"Her mama? Isn't she dead?" Chade asked, shocked.

"My point exactly. The bitch lied about everything, bro. She's been saying she has no family for years and here her mama comes knockin' my line down."

Malik proceeded to tell Chade everything that went down from the time he made it back to Cali. The look on his face was priceless because he couldn't believe what he was hearing. Chade had been busy as hell once he got back to work and didn't have much time to socialize. But hearing what Malik had been through, he was going to make it his business to get out for a breather with the guys.

"You mean to tell me the nigga she was creeping with was hiding drugs in yo' crib? Then on top of that, she tells the cops the shit was yours? That shit bogus as hell. I'm glad she's locked the fuck up because I would be tempted to push her ass into ongoing traffic for the stunt she pulled."

"On top of that, she had the nerve to call Toni and say she was my wife. Come to find out, the bitch logged into my T-Mobile app and went through my itemized bill to get the number. Making that call is what caused her to go to my people house acting a damn fool. Her muthafuckin' feelings were hurt."

"Yo, she didn't have no right to be mad. You had already sent the message that shit was over when you didn't answer her calls or went back to the house. On top of that, you sent eviction papers for her to get the fuck out ya crib. What more did she want?" Chade was livid. "I think you should call her OG back to see what she has to say. On some real shit."

"That's the same thing my mama said. I just want to wash my hands of the situation all together. It's not necessary in my opinion because Pops already moved her shit out. Speaking of moving, I'm going to need your help clearing out that crib so I can get it on the market."

"Where the hell you staying if not at the crib?" Chade questioned.

"My Pops copped me a crib not too far from them. The muthafucka is big as hell too. Actually, too big for just one nigga." Malik laughed. I'm gonna have to fast forward shit with Toni to get her out here permanently. I need a woman and a couple kids to turn it into a home. Right now, it's like a damn Airbnb when I'm there alone."

"Just let me know. I'll be there for whatever you need. You straight on bread, my nigga?"

Malik smiled at the mention of his finances. That was another reason he was eager to come talk to Chade. If there was anybody, he wanted dipping into his pockets, it would be his brother from another mother.

"Hell, I almost forgot about that shit. I need you to help me out." Malik told Chade about the trust fund and how he needed a reliable finance advisor.

"I can do that for you with no problem, bro. Down the line, you bet' not come to me talking shit about a female spending your shit without your knowledge either. As a matter of fact, don't tell nobody you even got that shit. Keep living like you've been as a muthafuckin' doctor. Your salary ain't chump change either, but it's not millionaire status."

Chade put Malik up on game and he got right to work coming up with a plan. By the time they were finished, it was a little after two and Chade was ready to call it a day. As he gathered his belongings, Malik's phone rang. The way his face lit up, it could only be one person.

"Hello, love."

"Hey. Sorry I missed your call. I put my phone on do not disturb and drowned myself in work. Is everything alright?" Toni sincerely asked.

"We'll talk about me when you get off work. How are you doing?"

"I'm alright for the most part. I've been maintaining to keep my sanity. Malik, I've been trying to remember what you said to me about Tangie, but I really want to find a way to help her. I haven't heard from her and I believe it's because she's running from the help I want to provide."

Toni sounded so sad and Malik didn't like it at all. He hated the distance between them because he couldn't go to her and wrap his arms around her. Family was very important to her and Malik understood that, but he didn't want Toni to burden herself with something she had no control over. To be honest, he didn't know what to say to her other than what he shared the other day.

"Babe, I want you to stop stressing over there. I wish there was more I can say, but I have nothing. Tangie will reach out sooner than later; I'm sure. In the meantime in between time, take care of Antonia. The last thing·I need is for you to worry yourself to the point of being sick."

"Yeah, I know. It's easier said than done and I'm trying. I added you to my favorites so your calls will come through even if I close out the rest of the world. I just thought I'd give you a call since you reached out. I'm going to get back to work while thinking about what I want to eat for lunch. Enjoy the rest of your day and thank you."

"You don't have to thank me, that's what I'm here for. I may not be there physically, but I'm a phone call away. If you need me beyond that, it's nothing for me to book a flight to be right by your side. Now, don't work too hard and make sure you call me when you're settled at home."

"I will," she said ending the call.

Malik went right to his Uber Eats app and ordered Toni lunch to be delivered to her job. He also ordered an Edible arrangement to put an extra smile on her face. Looking up from his phone, Chade stood smirking at his friend.

"Everything alright, in love-ass nigga?"

"Shut yo' ass up. Baylei got your ass out here proposing and shit, so who's in love?" Malik shot back.

"Yeah, you got me." Chade laughed. "There's a first time for everything and my baby put that love thang down on a real playa. For real though, what's going on with Toni?"

"She's worried about her cousin being deep in the streets on that shit. I'm trying to get her to understand she can't save someone who's not willing to participate in the rescue."

"Man, that's a tough one. I hope she clears her mind because she will drive herself crazy. You can lead the horse to water, but you can't make it drink. Toni is strong, bro. You just have to be there with her through it all." Chade threw his bag strap over his shoulder and grabbed his keys. "Let's get outta here so I can get out this monkey suit. We kickin' it tonight. I'll hit up the rest of the crew and text the location and time."

Malik walked out behind Chade a little differently than when he walked in. Getting his finances in check had him looking forward to his future like no other. On the flip side, he was also trying to figure out how to get Toni away from the sadness that was slowly eating away at her soul.

Chapter 7

"Denton!"

Ailani sat up on the hard-ass makeshift bed that she was trying to rest in. It had been a week since she was arrested and she had been moved to the Century Regional Detention Facility. The facility was filled with women that were doing time from petty crimes to hardcore murder. Ailani hadn't bathed since she got there because there were so many women trying to get at her in a sexual manner. She wasn't trying to go that route with any of them because she was all about the dick that spit up when it came.

"You have a visitor," the CO said loudly from the doorway.

Ailani didn't know who could've been there to see her. Honestly, she preferred no one come see her in a place she didn't want to be. Walking slowly down the hall with her hands cuffed behind her back, Ailani was searched before she was allowed entry to the visiting area. As she got further into the room, her heart started beating rapidly when she spotted the person waiting for her to join them.

"Lani, you look like shit." The person laughed.

Ailani didn't find the comment funny because being in jail wasn't a laughing matter. Of course, she would look like shit. She didn't have her makeup, hygiene products, a decent comb, or the clothes of her choice. Instead, she was forced to wear underwear and a state-issued suit with L.A. County Jail printed on the back.

"Why are you here, Dex? When I called, you didn't answer, so that meant you didn't want to be bothered."

"Sit yo' ass down because these damn rookie-ass cops looking this way," he snarled. "I didn't answer because I didn't want to talk over the phone. Now, what the fuck happened?"

Ailani eased into the chair and thought about how she was going to explain what happened to him. She knew telling the truth wasn't an option. There was enough heat on her as is. Ailani knew getting involved with Dex was a risk in itself, but she would do anything he asked to be a part of his life. Holding his drugs wasn't a big thing as long as he didn't ask her to do anything outside of that.

"My guy found the drugs and turned them over to the police. I got locked up for it because that's my place of residence. Now, I'm being charged with possession with intent to distribute. They are trying to throw the book at my ass."

Tears stung the back of her eyes as she sat back like a child being punished. Ailani told a half-truth and didn't mention the fact that the detectives have been hounding her to give up the guy in the surveillance video. She kept telling them the name of the guy was Mike, giving a false narrative about meeting him at a Walgreens and that she never thought he would give a false name.

"You gon' eat that charge and keep your mouth shut," Dex growled. "Don't tell them muthafuckas shit about who those birds belong to. Do you hear me? Bet' not one pig come sniffing around me or that's your ass, Lani! You can be touched in this muthafucka. Don't think you're safe. There's more to the bullshit story you just told, but it's all good. Your situation is beneath me and all on you. I'll make sure your books are loaded. That's about all I can do for you. Keep ya head up and don't let Trisha make you her bitch." Dex laughed again as if he told the joke of the year at Ailani's expense. His actions only turned her tears to anger.

"Do you know what it's like being in here? I have to be told when I can eat, sleep, and shit. When I'm able to go outside, I can only go as far as the gates allow. I feel like a damn caged dog and you're laughing. You are the reason I'm in this mess, Dex."

"No, you are the reason you're here. I didn't put a gun to your head in order for you to hold down my shit. Like every other woman that's in your position, it was the dick that demanded you to partic-ipate. He wins every time," he smirked. "I don't know why the caged bird sings, but bitch, you bet' not let me find out."

With that, Dex got up and walked out the door, not saying an-other word. Ailani understood then that Dex was only keeping her around for one thing; hiding his drugs. He didn't give a damn about her, so why was she protecting him from the police? Dex's lack of concern made her decision to rat his ass out easier. Ailani got up to go back to her cell when the CO walked over to her with a scowl on his face.

"Sit down. You're popular today. There's someone else here to see you."

Ailani eased back in the chair because she didn't fuck with anyone outside of Dex and Malik. Malik wasn't about to come in there because he was the reason she was sitting still with a load of problems. Whoever was coming needed to offer a bitch something to eat because her stomach was growling like a mug. The clicking of heels made Ailani turn her attention to the door. When she saw her mother and sister Yvonne walking toward her, she stopped breathing momentarily.

It had been years seen she'd laid eyes on anyone in her family. She left Arizona and ran to California when her mother tried to dictate her life. Living with her mother was no different than the way she was living in the very facility she sat in. The only difference was the fact the guards weren't shoving pills at her three times a day, seven days a week. Ailani didn't even know how her mother found her. Jail should've been the last place she thought to look.

"Surprised to see me, Ailani?" her mother asked, taking a seat with a scowl on her face.

"How did you find me?"

"That doesn't matter. You've been running for too long and you finally did something to sit your ass down for a minute. What did you do, Lani?"

Ailani looked everywhere but at her mother. She didn't want to get into why she was locked up.

"Answer the damn question. What's the point of staying quiet? We're here to try to see how we can help your stupid ass."

The sound of her sister's voice brought her right back to the conversation. She and Yvonne never got along, so Ailani didn't know why she was even talking. Ailani opened her mouth to cuss her out, but Alauna cut in right in time.

"No, we are not about to do this. Yvonne, sit back, be quiet, and let Lani answer the question. I'm not leaving here without finding out what I need to know," Alauna said, giving her daughter the floor to talk.

Adjusting herself in the seat, Ailani cupped her chin into her hand. "There were drugs in the house that belonged to Malik and I was arrested for it. There's nothing else to say about the matter."

"If that's the case, why the hell isn't Malik locked up too? See, I know more than you want me to know and wanted to see if you would come out with the truth. I called Malik, but he hasn't returned my calls—"

"You called him! Why would you do that? He doesn't even know you exist." The last part fell from Ailani's lips before she could stop the words from coming out. The look on both her mother and sister's faces told her shit was about to go from bad to worse.

"How are you in a whole relationship and the man just assume you were born like the son of Mary? Make it, make sense, sis," Yvonne said with pure attitude. "You probably told him we were dead or some shit."

Ailani started laughing. "I did, bitch! Now disappear because in my eyes, y'all are dead to me!" Ailani stood, sending the chair crashing behind her.

The loud noise caused the guard to rush over to see what was going on. "Is there a problem?"

"Yeah. Take me the fuck back to where I came from." Ailani put her hands behind her back and before long, the cuffs were locked in place. "Muthafuckas didn't give a damn about me then, so stop pretending to give a fuck now. Don't come back here," she shouted over her shoulder.

Alauna sat watching her youngest daughter being led away and felt a sense of guilt. She blamed herself for the night Ailani went out and someone slipped her a mickey at a party. Ailani was beaten, raped, and stayed months in a mental institution. She hadn't been right since. Alauna knew the reason she was sitting in a cell was because she stopped taking her medication. Malik was who she needed to speak with because even if she didn't know about Ailani's family, he was going to get the chance to meet her mama.

Chapter 8

It was almost the weekend, and Toni couldn't wait to get off work. There was a party later at Reynold's, a club that played house music all night. Mike Dunn and DJ Tony T always rocked the crowd. Tangie and Toni used to always go out and party the night away and she wanted to include her cousin in the fun. She looked at the clock, and it read two o'clock. That gave Toni three hours before she was set to get off to get in touch with Tangie. Going to her name in her phone, she pushed the contact and prayed she would answer. The man upstairs answered her prayers when the call connected.

"Hey, Cuz! What's going on?"

Tangie sounded so happy on the other end of the phone and that made Toni smile. Usually, she would sound as if the world was about to end and Toni didn't like that side of her. There was a small glimmer of hope that her cousin was ready to get her life on track. Tangie didn't sound high at all.

"I was calling to see if you wanted to go out with me and the girls tonight."

"Where you going, to Reynold's? I don't want to go to that up-pity place up north. You know house music is my thang."

"That's exactly where we're going. I want to dance the night away with you, boo." Toni was doing everything she could to get her cousin to accompany her to the club.

"I'm in! You coming to pick me up?" Tangie asked excitedly.

"Yeah, be at Auntie's house because I'll be over there when I get off work. You got anything to wear?"

"Now you know bummy is not my forte. I may get high, but my hygiene ain't never been questioned. I can still shit on these bitches out here."

Tangie was never one that couldn't dress. She stayed fly from head to toe. It didn't matter if she was dressed to the nines in a dress and heels, or a pair of jeans and a hoodie with Timbs on her feet. She was always clean. Toni was excited to go out and see her cousin in her element.

"I hear you, Cuz." Toni laughed. "I'll see you later and you better be there. How does six o'clock sound to you?"

"I'll be there for sure, Toni. I want to have some fun," Tangie said in a chipper voice.

Hearing her cousin's voice put Toni in a better mood than she'd been in over a week. Her mind opened up and she didn't struggle with her job the way she had been previously. The dark cloud that seemed to have been following her was gone after the conversation she'd had. There was a sense of promise and hope running through her body at that moment and she loved every minute of it.

Toni worked nonstop through the rest of her day and was so ready to leave so she would get ready for her Thursday night of house music. She had sent a text out for Baylei and Jordyn to meet at her aunt's house about eight o'clock. Whenever Toni went to Reynold's, there was no way for her to get up for work the next day. She put in for a personal day before she gathered her things to leave the office.

As Toni drove to her aunt's house, she had a jam session like she was at a Summer Jam concert. She was so elated to hang with her cousin that she was going faster than she'd ever done when getting off work. Traffic came to an abrupt halt and Toni groaned loudly as she slapped the steering wheel.

"This is some bullshit! Out of all days the traffic wants to be heavier than a big bitch in a lawn chair."

Toni took the opportunity to call Malik since she'd only talked to him briefly in the past week. When he answered, Malik was yelling out orders in the background. He came on the line talking very fast.

"Baby, I'll call you back. I'm extremely busy at the moment. I'll call you before you go to bed." With that, he hung up.

Malik and Toni had been missing one another like stray bullets. She had to admit, she missed him. The music started playing automatically and that took her mind off the traffic, somewhat. Once traffic started moving, Toni found out there was an accident holding up the traffic. Both cars were totaled and one was flipped upside down.

"Damn, I hope everyone is alright," she said lowly as she drove past the wreck. It took her an additional twenty minutes to pull into her aunt's driveway. Getting out of the car, Toni grabbed her overnight bag from the trunk. She already had it set in her mind that she would dress there. It didn't make sense to drive all the way to the suburbs when they would be partying a few miles from her aunt's place.

Toni rang the doorbell and waited patiently for someone to open the door. When Rob let her in, she hugged him after speaking and went right to the laundry room and placed her bag down. Her aunt was in the kitchen frying some chicken and her stomach growled loudly which caused Brenda to turn around.

"Hey, teetee's baby! Why you walking around hungry? Don't let me find out you don't have any food at home," she said with a frown.

"Now, you know if I don't have nothing else, I'm gonna have something to grub on." Toni washed her hands at the sink and grab a wing. "Has Tangie been here?" she asked, smacking.

"She's upstairs. I knew it was a reason she was in here singing and shit. Not that I'm complaining. I love seeing her like that. It's better than her walking around quiet and nervous. Where y'all going?"

"On 75th and Ingleside to Reynold's. I wanted her to get out and enjoy herself for a change. You know, get her away from the good for nothing folks she's been hanging around." Toni replied, reaching for another piece of meat.

"Get out of here! You know you only get one while I'm cooking. Once I'm done, you can eat as much as you like. Until then, get out of my kitchen."

"But we were talking, Auntie," Toni fake whined.

"Oh yeah. Well. go sit down somewhere and away from my food." Brenda chuckled and went back to stirring the cheese into the macaroni. "What do you know about these good for nothing folks, Toni?"

"I don't know anything, and that's a problem. One of these days I will find out though. I'll be right back."

Toni left out of the kitchen and went upstairs to find Tangie. When she got close to her room, the music could be heard coming from the other side of the door. Tangie was rapping her heart out to the tunes of DMX. She was reciting the lyrics from her heart and Toni felt as if she could hear her cousin sending out a message.

Wasn't long before I hit rock bottom
Niggas talking shit like damn look how that rock got him
Open like a window no more Indo look at a video
Sayin' to myself that could've been yo' ass on the TV
Believe me it could be done somethin's gots to give
It's got to change coz I've got a son
I've got to do the right thing for shorty
And that means no more getting high drinkin' forties
So I get back lookin' tight, slick again
Fake niggas jump back on my dick again
Nothin' but love for those that know how it feel
And much respect to all my niggas that kept it real
Kept a nigga strong kept a nigga from doin' wrong
Niggas know who they is, and this yo fuckin' song
And to my boo who stuck with a nigga through
All the bullshit you'll get yours because it's due
Ay yo I'm slippin' I'm fallin' I can't get up
Ay yo I'm slippin' I'm fallin' gots to get up
Get me back on my feet so I can tear shit up

Tangie stood in the mirror flat ironing her hair when Toni pushed the door open. She was wearing a tan halter shirt that wrapped around her flat stomach, showing off her navel piercing. The black distressed jeans had slits going down both pants legs and the tan Chucks on her feet set the outfit off. If one didn't know what Tangie went through on a daily, they wouldn't have found out that day. She looked damn good.

"You cute, Cuz!" Toni squealed as she moved further into the room.

"Stop acting like I'm new to this. I clean up well, huh?" Tangie smirked. "My insides may be fucked up, but my outer shell will never crack. That's what you're wearing?" she asked with her nose scrunched up.

"Hell nawl! What I look like going to the club looking like I just stepped out of a courtroom? You tried it though. I just wanted to come up here to see if you were bullshitting me about going out with me."

"I told you I was going. Get out and go get yourself together. As you can see, I'm readyyyyyyy!" Tangie danced around, swinging her arms over her head. "We're about to turn the fuck up!"

"It's the excitement for me! Let me go get cute. See you in a minute."

Toni bounced down the stairs and went to get her bag. She ran the iron over her pants and a few minutes later, she was in the shower washing away the smut of a day's work. After drying off, she moisturized her body and slipped on the black leather pants and a sheer off the shoulder blouse with a black bra underneath. The white and black heeled sandals showed off her white painted toes. Fingering her twenty-four-inch wavy lace front, she winked at herself in the mirror.

"Damn, girl, you fine," Toni said to herself as she did a light beat to her face. The nude tones had her glowing from every angle and she loved the person looking back at her. Putting the final touches on her makeup, Toni heard the doorbell and rushed to clean up.

Stepping into the hall, she could hear Baylei and Jordyn complimenting Tangie. Toni hoped like hell this outing and the ones that will come thereafter, would bring her cousin back to the life she once lived. She stood watching the interaction a bit before joining in on the praise. The first thing Toni saw was the big ass engagement ring glistening from the light.

"Dammmmmmnnn that ring poppin"!"

"Shut up," Baylei laughed while blushing. "This little thing ain't all that."

"Shid, that ring hittin'! You can get about two G's if you pawn that muthafucka," Tangie said. looking at her nails.

Her comment made everybody pause and brought a sense of awkwardness to the room.

Aunt Brenda walked in and broke the ice. The thoughts were the same all around. Tangie was thinking like an addict and Toni for one, didn't like it.

"Sit down so I can feed y'all before you leave here." She cut her eyes at Tangie and she hunched her shoulders in response.

"I'm sorry for saying that to you, Baylei. It's not my fault I can spot value without thought. If that nigga fuck up, I know just the spot for you to cash in on that muthafucka."

"Tangie, it's okay. You are still the same funny chick I met long ago. I don't expect you to change and lose your sense of humor," Baylei said with a smile. "Tangie, on some real shit though, I want you to reach out to me if you ever need to. I'll always be there for you and will help any way I can."

"Lei, I know that already. I just be out here working and trying to stay afloat. I'm good though. Look at me." Tangie got up and turned around so they could see her fully. "I don't look like there's anything wrong with me, right?"

"No, you look good *today*. What about tomorrow or the next day?"

"We can talk about this another day. I don't need to stress about how my life is right now. I love y'all and looking out for me is what y'all do. I appreciate it, I swear I do, but all I want to do is have a good time with my cousins. Is that too much to ask?

"No, it's not. I'm gonna hold you to that conversation too," Jordyn retorted as her plate was put in front of her.

The oven-baked macaroni, fried chicken, sweet peas, and garlic bread had Toni's mouthwatering. Her first spoonful of mac and cheese closed her eyes. That was one thing she absolutely loved; her aunt's cooking. They sat eating, laughing, and talking until everyone was good and full. After giving Linda hugs all around, the group left to get there night started.

Reynold's was jumpin' as usual and Toni was dancing before they entered the building. Security at the door noticed the crew and ushered them over. Baylei glanced in Toni's direction when she didn't move and nudged her. Toni knew if Reggie was there, LaZeric was already inside or on his way to the club.

LaZeric and Toni were in a relationship for years. Right before the death of her parents, he decided he wanted to be friends instead of lovers because he wasn't ready for a relationship. The breakup tore Toni up inside, but she got over the hurt and pushed forward to better herself. For months she blamed herself for not being enough for the man she loved. LaZeric told her many times his decision had nothing to do with her. Claiming he just couldn't give her the love she was seeking from him.

"Toni, I know you see me over here," Reggie's voice boomed over the chatter that was going on around them. "The party's inside."

"Nigga, don't holla my name like that! Fuck wrong with you?" Toni shot back.

"Get yo' stubborn ass over here and stop playing with me."

Tangie walked over to Reggie and the rest of them followed. She knew they were about to get in without paying and she was all for free shit. Ushering them inside, Reggie grabbed Toni's arm and whispered in her ear.

"Ya boy in there. Be nice to him, Tone."

"Fuck him! Thanks for giving me the heads up though," she said, snatching away before going inside.

Is it all over my face?

'Hell yeah!' the crowd shouted as the music to Loose Joints jam bumped through the speakers.

Baylei threw her hands in the air and Toni laughed because the night was about to be epic and she knew it. Making their way through the crowd, they headed straight to the bar. It had been a hot minute since they'd been to the club and nothing had changed about the vibe around them. Toni saw people she hadn't seen in a while, causing her to stop and give hugs and lots of what's up.

Jordyn lucked up and found an empty table and they sat down immediately. It didn't last long because the next beat dropped and it was nonstop dancing from that point on. Toni was sweating, which caused her to wipe her forehead with the napkin that she had wrapped around her drink. Everybody was having a good time and the outing was much needed. A presence was felt behind her and her body stiffened when she felt a strong bulge on her ass.

"You lookin' good as fuck tonight." Toni tried to turn around but the tightness around her waist wouldn't allow her to. "I've missed you, Toni."

Wiggling out of LaZeric's grasp, Toni spun around quickly and glared at him. She headed for the exit because she knew if she voiced what she had to say in the club, everyone within earshot would hear her tear his down and she didn't need anyone in her business. With steam coming out of her ears, Toni pushed the door open with so much force that it slammed against the wall with a bang.

"Slow down, Tee. Why are you so mad?" LaZeric asked.

"Fuck you! How the hell you just gon' push up on me talking about how much you miss me, LaZeric? That's the bullshit I'm not about to play with you. Keep the same energy you had when that friend shit fell from your lips. My feelings aren't to be played with and that's exactly what you're trying to do."

"I'm not trying to play with your feelings. When I told you I wasn't ready to be in a relationship, I meant that. It doesn't take from how I feel about you though. I do miss you and that's on everything I love. The last thing I'd ever want to do is hurt you. So, I walked away from the 'us' part of our relationship. Toni, you will always have a place in my heart."

The only thing Toni heard was "the last thing I want to do is hurt you". "Five years, six months, fifteen days, we were together! You have a whole bitch and you say the last thing you wanted to do was hurt me! After you said you wasn't ready, humph. Well, let me fill you in on something; that's *exactly* what you did. I guess the 'at least not with you' was silent, huh?" When he didn't say anything, Toni kept going. "Go do you because I'm definitely doing me.

There's no reason for you to be in my face trying to wear me down because it won't work."

"You can do you to a certain extent. Don't get carried away with that shit. It won't last," he smirked. "You know how far to take the bullshit."

Toni laughed because LaZeric was still trying to stake claim to someone he walked away from. The loyalty, honesty, and continuous love she dished out weren't enough for him to take what they had to the next level. He was well aware that she was a great catch, but wanted her to wait for him to be ready. That shit was hilarious to her.

"Nah, I can do what the fuck I want, when I want, and with whomever I want. There's nothing you can do or say about it. You made your choice. Don't come to me talking like you're my man. Go spit those rules to the woman you chose over the great one. You would never find another me and I stand on that shit."

Toni walked away leaving LaZeric standing outside the club. Getting a fresh drink, she went back to the table she left before she was interrupted. Jordyn walked toward her and Toni shook her head to stop her from asking any questions. They enjoyed the rest of the night and left smiling; everyone   except Toni. She was in her feelings about seeing LaZeric.

***

After dropping Tangie off at her aunt's house, Toni jumped on the Dan Ryan and headed home. The anger came out freely as she drove and thought about the situation she had with her ex. She hated seeing him because the interaction had her heart arguing with her mind. The love she had for LaZeric was everlasting, but they were better off being friends. No one had ever been hurt to the point of depression from losing a friend.

Toni's phone vibrated between her legs and her aunt's name was on display.

"Hey, auntie. What are you doing up so late?"

"I'm up waiting on Tangie to get in. I thought I saw your car pull in the driveway about ten minutes ago."

"You did. I dropped Tangie off at your door, Auntie. She should be in the house."

"Tangie never came in this house, Toni. I don't know where she went. Let me call that girl," Brenda huffed.

"I'm about to get off the expressway and come back."

"No, go home, baby. I'm going to track her down and keep you posted. This is how Tangie do all the time."

"Are you sure?" Toni asked.

"Yes, I'm sure. Call me when you get home and drive safely. I love you."

"I love you too, Auntie."

Toni erased her mind of her ex and thoughts of Tangie took its place. Shaking off all thoughts, she turned on the radio and let the music guide her home. When she pulled into her driveway, Toni called Tangie, but of course she got the voicemail. Instead of blowing her phone up, she gathered her overnight bag and went into the house.

Going straight into the bathroom after dropping her bag on the floor, Toni started the shower to get the water nice and hot. After stepping out of her clothes, she got in and let the water release the stress that was built up in her body. After washing thoroughly, Toni got out and wrapped a towel around herself. The cool air from the air conditioner sent a shiver up her spine. As she pulled a pair of boy shorts and a tank over her body, the doorbell sounded.

Glancing at the big clock on her bedroom wall that read one o'clock in the morning, Toni wondered who the hell could be at her house unannounced. The first thought that came to mind was to allow whoever was at her shit to stay on the other side of the door. Hoping they would get the picture; Toni lifted her leg to get in bed when the doorbell started chiming repeatedly. Thinking something was wrong, she rushed out of the room and down the stairs. She peeked out the side window and groaned before turning the locks.

"Why are you here, LaZeric?" she asked with her hand on her hip.

"I need to talk to you. Can I come in?"

Toni knew if she let him in, talking would've been the last thing they did. She wasn't falling for LaZeric's bullshit that night. The thought of Malik made her lady parts tingle and she knew her ex wasn't going to cross the threshold.

"No, that's not going to happen. We can talk right here. What's so important that you had to come over at this time of the morning?"

"I knew you were still awake because you just left the club. I've never had to talk outside the house when I come here, Toni. Move out the way so I can sit down," LaZeric said, trying to push his way past her.

"Ummmm, that's a hard no for me. Speak on what you have to say so you can go the fuck home to your woman. You're not coming in my shit. As a matter of fact—" Toni walked out onto the porch and closed the door behind herself. "We can sit right out here."

Toni sat down in the chair in the corner of the porch and LaZeric stood in front of her, leaning on the post. He stared at her with so much intensity that Toni felt kind of uncomfortable under his scrutiny. The way he was looking over her body and trying to figure her out had Toni laughing on the inside. Times had changed drastically since she was with him.

"What's really good, Tee? Why you being so standoffish with me?"

Cocking her head to the side, Toni looked at him like he was an alien or something. She knew damn well he wasn't standing before her acting as if it was noon. LaZeric could've waited until the sun came up to discuss this crap because she wasn't about to go into something he caused.

"You're not going to answer my questions?"

"First of all, I'm good. Secondly, I'm not being standoffish. Anything else?" she asked snidely.

"Stop playing with me, man. You treating me like I killed yo' dog or something. In the end, we're still friends."

"Are you finished, LaZeric? I need to get some sleep for work tomorrow. You're preventing me from doing that."

"Whatever. I wanted to let you know that I saw Tangie on 68th and Indiana at the drug spot. What the hell is she doing over there?"

"Tangie has been going through some shit. I'm glad you let me know where she's been hanging out because I was going to ride around to find out on my own. Thank you."

"I didn't know she was on that shit. I told her to get the fuck away from there and took her to Brenda's crib. Toni, let me know when she comes up missing so I can go get her ass. She don't need to be over there."

"Tell me something I don't know. There's only so much I can do when it comes to my cousin. She's grown and is going to do what she wants regardless of what anybody says to her. If you want to keep dragging her away from what she wants to do, by all means, do that. I won't tell you not to. My question to you is, why didn't you say that off top? Why beat around the bush about what you really wanted to say?"

"It don't matter. Go inside and get some sleep. I'll talk to you later and you better answer the phone," LaZeric said as Toni got up to go in the house.

"Good luck with that," she said, leaving him standing outside before slamming the door.

She watched as he raised his hand hesitantly to knock on the door, but thought better of it and walked away and got in his car. LaZeric backed out of the driveway slowly and Toni rested her back on the door closing her eyes.

"Damn, I love that man. Not enough to be his fool though. Goodnight, LaZeric. Our ship has sailed and there is no coming back from it."

Making sure the door was locked, Toni went upstairs to sleep away the pain that ached at her heart.

Chapter 9

Since the day Ailani got caught with the drugs in her house, Dex tried his best to go about his days as usual. The shit was hard because every time he saw a cop, he became paranoid as hell. Ailani knew what type of nigga he was and knew better than to open her mouth about where the birds came from. He meant what he said to her the day he went to visit her. If any heat came his way, she wouldn't be safe in that cell.

Dex got out of his cocaine white Jaguar XF and made his way into the barbershop.

"What up, Dex?" his barber Deon yelled out as he put the finishing touches on the client's head in the chair. "I'll be with you in a few minutes, dawg."

"Take your time. I have a little bit of time today. How's things shakin' wit you?"

"I can't complain. These knuckleheads out in the street gon' make me forget I changed my life for the better."

"What happened?" Dex asked seriously.

"Man, lil niggas was trying to break in my shit right outside. I went out with my three-eight and they ran the fuck off. Come to find out, they took their asses to 63rd and Cottage and hijacked an old lady. Muthafuckas took her money, phone, the car, and still shot her before pulling off. When I saw that shit on the news, I wanted to cry. That woman didn't deserve that shit, man."

"Damn, that's fucked up. These folks out here don't care about nothing nowadays. There's no guidance, and they don't have any sense of direction out here. On top of that, they don't value life anymore. It's a kill or be killed mindset out here and that shit is dangerous for any and everybody," one of the guys said, putting his input in on the situation.

"Now, had you blown their heads off for messing with ya shit, you would've been the one locked up. How's the lady they jacked doing? Have they said?" Dex asked.

"Nah, all they reported on the news was that she's in critical condition. Her car was found on 119th somewhere, but the lil niggas was nowhere in sight. Somebody gon' tell on their ass because that was somebody's mama. They better catch 'em before they run up on the right somebody. Find them in the morgue fuckin' around on that dumb shit."

Mark took the cape from around his client's neck and motioned for Dex to come have a seat. Dex went to Mark to get his hair cut once a week like clockwork. Krew Kuts was one of Dex's businesses, but no one knew he was the owner. He let Mark take over as if it was his because he needed the spot to wash his illegal money.

When Mark finished cutting him up and getting his beard right, Dex paid him like any other customer would and left. He went straight home and was greeted with tiny squeals of happiness from his four-year-old twins Delilah and Deliya. The sound of their little feet running from the playroom was music to Dex's ears. He moved into the middle of the room and his eyes lit up at the sight of his girls running towards him.

"Daddy, you home!"

Scooping both of his babies into his arms, Dex gave them kisses simultaneously, causing them to giggle. The twins were his prized possessions and he loved them more than life itself. Everything Dex did was for his daughters. They were the reason he even came home at night. Their mother, Melissa, was just that; their mother. She was taken care of by Dex off the strength of her being the mother of his kids. In his mind, she was just a surrogate that birthed them just for him.

There was never a relationship between the two. Dex just got caught up in the heat of passion and a drunken night, the results being his seeds traveled to the egg and succeeded. He couldn't ask her to terminate the pregnancy, so he did what he had to do and prepared for his child to enter the world.

Melissa knew Dex didn't love her, but she would rather her kids have their father in their lives than not. She knew he was outside of the house doing whomever, whenever, and that was fine by her. As long as he took care of home, that's all she worried about. When the time was right, they would be co-parenting anyway. The only difference would be they wouldn't be living underneath the same roof.

"Where's your mama?" Dex asked, walking further into the house.

"She in the kitchen making chicken nuggets," Delilah sang.

"Yeah, and French fries," Deliya added.

"Is that what y'all wanted?"

"Yep," both of them said, nodding their heads up and down.

Dex entered the kitchen and Melissa was bent over, reaching into the oven. The view was a sight to see from where he was standing, but there was nothing he could do about the way his dick swelled in his pants. Melissa wasn't coming off the pussy for him. They were roommates raising two beautiful girls. Nothing more, nothing less.

"Hey, Lissa. How you doing today?"

"I'm alright. You staying in for the night? I have something to do and wanted to know if I had to take the girls to my mom's," she said over her shoulder.

Dex stood quietly, wondering what she had to do all of a sudden. He always found himself questioning Melissa when she was heading out, but she never did the same to him. He wasn't tripping about her staying quiet about where he went or had been. That shit didn't work for her though. She still had to answer to him.

"Where you going?" he asked.

"None of your business. I don't be all in your shit, so stay out of mine. When you come and go, there's nothing being said on my part. Give me the same courtesy. Don't worry about it. I'll take my kids to their grandma for the night." Melissa slammed the door of the oven and attempted to walk past him.

"Don't storm out of here, Lissa. I just asked a simple question. My kids are staying right here. I have no problem sitting with them while you go on your thot mission. Tell that nigga you need some bread to go with that head while you at it."

"Why are you so worried about what I'm doing? Don't you have your slew of women outside that door?" Melissa asked, pointed at the wall adjacent to the door.

"That's beside the point. If you want to build something with the next nigga, he should be providing for your ass at his crib. I pay the cost to be the boss in this muthafucka."

"I work every day, Dexter. You sometimes seem to forget that you take care of Delilah and Deliya. You don't do shit for Melissa Santiago, baby. Every dime you give me for them, is used for that purpose alone. What's left over goes in *their* account that *I* opened on their behalf. Don't come for me because I've never needed you or your money. I don't know why there always has to be a disagreement when I want to leave this house."

"I'm not trying to hear all that. Feed my babies and go about your business," Dex said, leaving her mad in the kitchen.

He sat with his daughters, who were watching cartoons while waiting for their food. He took that opportunity to go upstairs to take a shower. When he got to his bedroom, he turned on the TV and undressed. A breaking news story came on, causing him to give the TV his undivided attention.

"The LAPD is looking for this man today. He's wanted for questioning at this time. If there's anyone that has a tip on his whereabouts, please contact LAPD Crime Division. We will have more on this story as details come in. Back to you, Rachel.

"Ain't this a bitch! Ailani's stupid ass didn't know there were cameras around that muthafucka! Now my damn face plastered across the damn airwaves. I'm gonna kill that bitch!"

Dex was hot under the collar and the only thing he could do was lay low. Staying inside with the twins was the best thing for him at the moment. He showered and put on a pair of basketball shorts with a T-shirt and went back downstairs. His babies were sitting at the table eating their chicken nuggets and fries. Melissa was nowhere in sight. She was probably in her room getting ready for her night out.

"Is it good?" he asked, taking a seat in one of the chairs at the table.

"Yes. You want some of mine?" Deliya asked, holding out a nugget.

"No, baby. You eat so you can be big and strong," Dex said pulling his phone from his pocket. He sat tapping away on his phone while periodically glancing up at his daughters.

Dex: Get at that bitch tonight! She's holding back information and got my face circulating on TV and shit. Make her tell you everything.

Trisha: Aight. If she doesn't talk, you know I'm beating her ass.

Dex: Do what you gotta do. Make sure she knows talking is not up for discussion. She better keep her mouth closed.

Trisha: What are you going to do though? They have your picture out there and they're looking for you.

Dex: Don't worry about all that. I'm going to take care of it. Let me know what happens on your end.

Trisha: Bet.

Dex was nervous as fuck on the inside. He needed to contact his lawyer to see what his next move would be.

The sound of Melissa's heels clicking on the hardwood floor brought his attention off his phone and in her direction. Baby girl was looking good as hell in a multi-colored maxi dress with a pair of heeled sandals of the same color. Her makeup was flawlessly done and her hair was no longer in the bun from earlier. It flowed down her back in big curls and framed her face perfectly.

"Give Mommy a kiss. I'll see y'all in the morning." Melissa kissed both girls on their cheeks and stood to leave.

"You're not coming in until morning?" Dex vexed.

"No, I'll be back tonight. I said that because they will be asleep when I get back. Is there anything else you would like to interrogate me about?"

"Nah, I'm good. Have fun, and don't do anything I wouldn't do." He laughed.

"In that case, I can do whatever because that's how you get down, right?"

Melissa left before Dex could hit her with a comeback. He wanted to follow her out the door, but he had other shit to worry about. Instead, he sat admiring his daughters and hoped he could get out of the jam he found himself in.

Chapter 10

The detectives kept coming to talk to her and she was tired of all the questioning. How many times did she have to tell them the guy's name that was on the camera? Ailani was starting to sound like a robot on repeat messing around with them. She didn't know what else to tell them.

After she was taken back to her cell after the long interrogation, Ailani was exhausted. She fell asleep until chow time and the food was nasty as usual. She'd lost a lot of weight in the short period of time of being locked up because she refused to eat the shit they served every day. Most of the time she only ate when her body felt as if it was going to give out from lack of nourishment.

Not being able to stomach the food any longer, Ailani dumped her tray and headed back to her cell to lie down. Hearing a commotion behind her, she didn't look back because she'd learned to mind her business. If she acted like she didn't see anything, it was less likely that she'd be questioned about anything that happened. That day she wished she had looked over her shoulder.

When Ailani stepped into her cell, she was pushed from behind. Her head hit the floor with a thud and she saw stars. As she tried to get to her feet, Ailani was forced back down by someone putting their foot on her neck.

"How the fuck did the police get an image of Dex?"

Hearing Dex's name mentioned in an all-women's prison sent a shiver down Ailani's spine. The thought of news about Dex reaching the inside had her damn near ready to piss herself. The detectives were just harassing her about giving him up that very day and she refused to rat him out. But here she was being assaulted and she was innocent. She did what he asked and kept her mouth closed. Why was this happening to her? That was all she thought about instead of responding.

"Oh, so you can't talk? Then I guess I'll force you to do so."

Ailani was kicked, punched, and dragged by her hair until she couldn't see in front of her.

"Okay, I'll tell you. Please don't hit me anymore," she got out in barely a whisper. "Malik had cameras outside the house and he must've turned them over to the police. I didn't know they were there until the detectives came asking me who the person was in the picture. I gave them a fake name so they wouldn't go after Dex. I'm sorry. I didn't say anything," Ailani wailed.

"Tell me everything you know on this Malik person. Since he wants to talk to the police, his ass gon' get dealt with too."

Ailani started singing like a canary. She didn't know where he was living after he moved out of the house they shared, but she gave up his parents' address and his place of employment. That was all she could give on him. Even with Ailani giving up the information, she was beaten repeatedly until she blacked out. She could hear someone say, "Let's go, Trish," before she lost consciousness.

***

Waking up in the infirmary was a chore of its own. Ailani felt like she had been hit by a garbage truck. Her body ached all over and it hurt to swallow the saliva that kept building up in her mouth. She couldn't open her eyes and her head was banging. Someone came in and she started shaking from not knowing who was in the room with her. Turning her head toward the sound, a hand touched her shoulder.

"Miss Denton, it's Detective Lemon. Who did this to you?"

"I'm not talking as long as I'm in here. That's what got me in this situation in the first place. I need protection," Ailani struggled to say. "He told me I can be touched and looked what happened. I was beat the fuck up."

"Who is he? I can't help you if you don't tell me."

"I only know him by Dex. He had some girls beat the shit out of me. The person responsible is Trish. To get to Dex, all you have to do is look at the visitor log. I've had three visitors since being here and he was the only male. Get the logs and you have your man. Now, what are y'all going to do for me? If I stay here, I'm going to get killed." Tears made their way out the corners of Ailani's swollen eyes and it burned like hell. She fought through the pain as she continued to talk to the detective.

"The drugs didn't belong to Malik or myself. Dex asked me to hold onto the drugs for him. If you test the packaging and the duffle bag, you will see that I've never touched any of that shit. The only reason I told him I would hold it is because he threatened to kill me. I'm not a drug dealer." Ailani brought the tears out more as she tried to get the pity of the detective. Whatever she had to do to get out of the predicament she was in, she was willing to do it.

"Why didn't you tell us this when we asked before?"

"Which part of he said he would kill me don't y'all understand? As you can see, his reach is long if he got somebody in here to beat me like this! I'll testify. I'll wear a wire. Whatever you need me to do. I won't be safe until he's locked away and off the street. Just help me the way I'm trying to help you. I'm not safe in here!"

Ailani's cries echoed off the walls in the room and the detective felt her pain. He got on his phone and made a call to get her into protective custody. It was going to take her a while to heal because she was beaten pretty badly. Detective Lemon was anxious to get to the big fish so he could throw the book at his ass. But he had to make sure Miss Denton was safe first.

Detective Lemon was able to get an ambulance to escort Ailani to the hospital. They had guards at her door so she couldn't leave and no one could enter. After getting her settled, he and his partner went over the visitor log and the name Dexter Hinton was on the top of the list. After typing his name into the data base, he saw that Dexter, a.k.a. Dex, had a very long rap sheet. He actually had a warrant for his arrest for murder and plenty of drug charges that he'd done time for. There were many addresses listed for him and they were going out to apprehend him sooner rather than later.

Once the doctor cleared Ailani for discharge, she only had bruising of her eyes and ribs, along with a gash in her head that required a few stitches. She also had a mild concussion, but she was good to go. Detective Lemon led her to his car and drove to the next destination, which was an apartment the department used for protective custody.

"You are not to leave the premises. There's someone watching at all times, so don't try to be sneaky. You are not to call anyone or reveal your whereabouts. As far as anyone knows, you are still in jail. Don't make me regret helping you, because your ass will be right back in a cell getting your ass kicked again. Do you hear me?"

Ailani nodded her head yes as she sat holding her head in her hands. "Can I have something for my headache?" she asked.

Detective Lemon gave her the medication the doctor prescribed and got up to leave the apartment. Ailani took an eight hundred milligram of ibuprofen and stretched out on the couch. She grabbed the remote and searched for the on button through the small slits of her eyes. She turned the TV on and the first thing she saw was the picture of Dex along with his full name and the fact that he was wanted for murder. Ailani quickly turned the channel and settled for a true crime show on the ID Channel. She watched the documentary for about fifteen minutes before the medication put her into a deep slumber.

Chapter 11

"Hey, love. How you doing?"

Malik smiled in the camera as he looked at Toni. Facetime had been their way of communicating and in his mind, it wasn't enough. With both of them working hard and the extra stress that was in their lives, picking up the phone to check on one another was about all they'd had the chance to do. They sent "missing you" gifts and shit like that, but it wasn't the same as their usual conversations.

"I'm maintaining." The smile on her lips didn't reach her eyes and Malik didn't like that at all. "What about you?"

"Well, I know we have been quick texting and talking briefly, but baby, you look so sad. What's the matter? I'm not okay if you're not, so we need to get to the root of what's bothering you and get your energy up to par."

"I'm alright. Nothing has changed with Tangie, and—"

"We talked about this, Antonia. All you can do is pray about that. There's nothing more outside of that."

"I know. We went out on Thursday and she had a good time. Didn't get high one time and we were out for damn near five hours. Soon as I dropped her off, she was right back in the streets! Helping her is my main focus outside of work and it's taking a toll on me."

"That's all the reason for you to take a breather and allow her to come to you when she's ready. I'm not saying don't check on her or abandon her, but you're going to have to step back. This isn't good for your mental, baby."

A tear fell from her eye and she hurried to swipe it away as she turned away from the camera. "I try to bury myself in work to keep my mind off everything that's going on around me. It's not working. I miss you, Malik. I wish you were here to wrap your arms around me."

"Toni, I wish I could come to you at this time. I've been busy at the hospital, but that's not all that's been occupying my time." Malik filled Toni in on what had been going on in sunny California. The expressions on her face kept changing with every word he spoke. When he finished, she was speechless.

"Malik, I want you to be careful because something isn't right with that woman. To be honest, I think you should call her mother and give her a chance to say whatever it is she's so eager to say. If I'd known this earlier, you would've been found out all there is to know about Miss Ailani. There's a lot about her you don't know and it's about time you find out. The time is now, baby."

"Yeah, my mama and Chade said the same thing. I'm going to bite the bullet and call her when I get off the phone with you. Just so you know, miss you too, Miss Juicy Pussy," Malik said, licking his lips.

"You don't miss me. You miss my kitty. All you got to do is tell me that you want to feel the walls of my love box squeezing your strong muscle."

Malik's joint swelled in his pants and the image of their first night together played in his head.

"Close your mouth, baby. I'm going to make sure you're taken care of soon. I need to do the sexual tango with you too."

"I'm going to make sure you can get in even if I'm not home. I'll text the address and when you're ready, show up. That would be the best surprise a man could ever get. An unexpected visit from the woman of his dreams. Speaking of you coming to see me—" Malik paused. "I'm not feeling this long-distance shit. I need you with me morning, noon, and night. We have to come up with a master plan because there's too much space and not enough opportunity between us."

"Don't remind me, Malik. Right now isn't the time for me to pack up and leave. You know what I'm dealing with. I can make a promise to come out every other weekend until we can take that step. What you think?"

"Why not every weekend, Toni? I will fly you out with no problem. Long as I can love on you up close and personal," Malik expressed how he was feeling. and it swelled Toni's heart.

"I can't promise you every weekend, but I will make sure I see you often as possible. You better be careful because the way I've been sexually deprived, I may put a baby in your ass."

They both laughed and talked for a little while longer before Malik explained that he had to go so he could clean out the house and put it on the market. He had two and a half hours before he had to pick up the U-Haul truck and meet his guys at the house. His first stop was to the Home Depot to get a key made for Toni. After getting the duplicate, he went straight to FedEx and had the key mailed overnight.

In Malik's mind, Toni was it for him. They may not have known each other long, but he knew what he felt for her was real. Once he closed all the negativity out of his life, he would be able to concentrate on his goal and his woman fully.

He pulled into his parents' driveway and sent his father a text to come outside. Malik Sr. walked out of the house looking like a forty-year-old when he was actually in his mid-fifties. Malik was a younger version of his father and they could pass for brothers rather than father and son.

"My boy, what's shakin'?"

Malik laughed until tears fell from his eyes at his father talking like he was young. "I'm gon' need you to talk like you got a grown-ass son." Malik continued to laugh. "I'm cool, Pops. What about you?" Malik said, backing out of the driveway once his father was seated comfortably.

"I'll be a lot better when this crazy shit you're going through is over."

"It's done. After I get this house cleaned out, I'm moving on to bigger and better things."

"Speaking of cleaning the house out, I have a couple people that's ready to purchase the furniture and take it off your hands. I knew you didn't need any of it, so I didn't bother asking. I got that shit off for you. There's no sense in putting it in storage when you can make a profit."

Malik listened to his father and what he'd done made a lot of sense.

"I'll take the truck and help them unload, then I'll deposit the funds into your account. You can pay me by taking me out to eat at M'Dears."

"Thanks, Old Man. I can do that. You are always there for me and I appreciate all that you've done. I can't thank you enough. Without you, I don't know where I would be right now. I love you, Dad."

"Get yo' ass outta here with all that soft-ass shit. That's how your ass got duped by that silly-ass girl you called your woman for years. Son, from here on out, I want you to put your foot down and not allow any woman to run over you."

"You mean like Ma do you," he said, giving his father a quick glance.

"Nigga, that's not the same thing. Yo' mama is invested. She earned the right to boss my ass around and I welcome that shit. We have thirty years under our belts. When you get to that level of love, come holla at'cha boy. Until then, you still in the toddler stage of living."

Malik and his father got out and entered the building to get the keys for the truck. He wanted the type of love his parents had for one another and one day, he would achieve that goal. There was nothing that could tear them apart. They bickered here and there, but Malik never witnessed any type of disrespect from either of them. He was sure they had many ups and downs, but the important part about it was they never did it in front of Malik.

"I'll see you at the house. I hope your friends are there on time because I have a lot to do today," Malik Sr. said, climbing into the truck.

"You know my people always show up on time. Let me take that back. Chade may be late, but he will be there." Malik laughed.

"Chade's going to be late for his own funeral, so he gets a pass. Drive safely, son."

Malik waited until his father pull off before he followed him out of the lot. It took them four hours to load the truck. They took a couple of breaks to eat, smoke, and bullshit, but the job was done. Malik Sr. took off as soon as the last of the items were loaded on the truck, leaving Malik, Chade, Samir, and Ahmad in attendance.

"Where the hell is Vincent? I haven't heard from him in a minute," Ahmad asked.

"That nigga in Chicago under Chaya. She got his ass wide the fuck open, and they better be using protection." Everybody laughed because he had the most serious expression on his face.

"You better concentrate on your own shit. How's Baylei doing anyway?" Samir asked.

"Samir, you know damn well you don't care about Baylei. But she's good. I miss her lil fine ass. We're trying to figure out when she'll be moving to the palace so I can caress her ass all night."

"That long distance shit is for the birds. I don't know how the hell y'all do it. Especially you, Chade." Samir said shaking his head.

"The shit is hard, but I didn't put a ring on her finger to fuck her over. Believe me when I tell you, pussy is still being thrown in my direction. I'm working hard like a superhero blocking that shit at every turn. When I expressed my love for Baylei, I meant every word. There isn't another woman on earth for me."

Malik stood up because the same black vehicle had circled the block three times, and that was unusual for the neighborhood they were in. When he was about to address it with his boys, the passenger window lowered and the barrel of a gun was exposed. Before Malik could react, shots rang out and everyone took cover trying to avoid getting hit. The screeching of tires was heard, and then there was silence.

"Y'all good?" Samir asked, getting to his feet.

Everybody got up, brushing off their clothes; except Malik.

"Malik!" Chade shouted as he rushed to his friend's aide. "He's hit! Call for an ambulance." Chade snatched his shirt off his back and applied pressure to Malik's side to slow down the bleeding.

Meesha

Chapter 12

Sitting in her office eating a roasted turkey sandwich with a bag of plain Lays potato chips, Baylei was trying to eat quickly before diving back into the work that was piled on her desk. Her eyes were tired from going back and forth from the computer to the lines of the drawings she was working on. There was a light knock on her door before it slowly opened and Wes peeked his head in.

"Hey, you busy?"

"Nah, just taking a quick break to eat. I worked up an appetite. What you got for me?" Baylei asked, taking a sip of her cranberry juice.

"I don't have any work for you." Wes laughed. "I came in to talk to you about various things. You got time?" Baylei nodded her head and motioned for Wes to take a seat. "First, I want to say, you are exceeding my expectations. Not saying you wasn't good when you first started working for me, but you are phenomenal now."

"Awwww, thank you, Boss. I'm glad I've made you proud. I take pride in the work I do. It's a pleasure working for a company that runs smoothly without hassle. I consider you and the team family, and that's hard to come by."

"Well, us coloreds have to stick together and make shit shake for us. I got ya back through thick and thin; believe that. Baylei, you will go far in your career. Speaking of your career, how's things going with you and Chade? I mean, you are here in Chicago, and he is in Cali. Both of you are working hard and striving with it. But, y'all are in a long-distance engagement. How does that work?"

Baylei sat back, releasing air from her lungs as she closed her eyes slowly. "I've been thinking about this very thing for a while now and truthfully speaking, I don't know. I mean, in the short period of time we've known one another, I love him just as much as he loves me. That's the reason I accepted the proposal."

"What's the problem then? You should be with your soon- to-be husband, Baylei. Y'all too far apart to build anything together.

The last thing you want is to get comfortable being apart. A partnership takes both parties doing shit together. You don't want to give any leg room for Chade to dip in another honey pot."

Wes wasn't saying anything Baylei hadn't already thought about. Hearing it from someone else made everything real. She had to face the truth about the situation she was in and it was no better time to voice it than to a man that was willing to listen and give positive feedback. Baylei played around with wording in her head and was becoming frustrated because none of it made sense, so she just let her thoughts flow from her lips while she was willing to express herself.

"The problem is, I have a career to think about. You know, the one you just told me I'm kicking ass doing. Wes, I can't up and leave what I love. I worked too hard to get where I am and I don't think I could ever work for anyone else. You are the Boss of Bosses, and there's nobody else out there like you."

"I get that, and I appreciate the high praise. You deserve to be happy with your career and in life. Don't let your career goals stop you from experiencing a love you deserve, Baylei. You can create anywhere; not just in Chicago."

Baylei was quiet as she listened to Wes. It was a little too long for him because he exhaled and propped his elbows on top of her desk. Looking into her eyes, he smiled.

"Baylei, I've grown to love you like a little sister and I want the best for you. There's things in my business that I haven't disclosed to anyone in this building and you will be the first." Wes sat back and cleared his throat. "As you know, I'm a businessman. I take pride in everything I do and I'm damn good at it."

"Where are you going with this, Wes? I know all of that about you already. Get to the shit I don't know." Baylei laughed.

"I've been working on expanding King's Architect for over a year and I finally got it up and running. It has actually been doing very well for the past six months. With that being said, I have a proposition for you. I don't want you to accept or decline today. I want you to think on it before giving your response." Wes paused and once again, Baylei was silent.

"The new branch is located in Los Angeles. I need someone to oversee the business, just as I'm doing here. There's no one better for the position than you, Baylei. I know how passionate you are about your work, and you can still create your masterpieces. It just wouldn't be mandatory for you to do so. You would be able to step in wherever you fit, but the position is breezy. Working from home when you want is optional, but on the table as well."

Baylei's eyes grew to the size of golf balls, but she was utterly speechless. Wes always came through for her and he wasn't short-stopping that day. He actually solved her dilemma about being so far away from Chade.

"The annual salary for that position is one hundred forty-nine thousand a year. With you making close to seventy thousand now, I'm willing to bring your salary to an even two hundred thousand to compensate the work I know you will still create in spite of your position. You will also still get your bonuses for the projects you complete."

Baylei could no longer hide her emotions and the tears flowed down her cheeks. Her mother always said she would get her blessing in return tenfold. Baylei didn't expect them to come flowing in abundantly. She was happier with the fact that she would be with Chade than with the amount of money the position would add to her bank account. Wiping her tear-stained face with a Kleenex, she said,

"Thank you for considering me, and I'm sorry for crying like a baby. This is the perfect opportunity for me to be with Chade." Baylei beamed with happiness as she blew her nose.

"Fuck Chade! You about to be in the big league making that paper." Wes laughed.

"To be honest, I don't need the money," Baylei said sheepishly. "Between me and you, Noah's punk ass left me well off. I'll just say, he's still apologizing from the grave. I don't have to work another day of my life if I don't want to, but I love what I do and I will continue doing just that until I'm tired."

"That's what the fuck I'm talking about! You deserve that shit, Baylei. Don't allow anybody to say you don't. The things that man put you through was hell for anyone to encounter. Grow from the experience and do not let what happened make you feel guilty."

'Does this look like a face that shows a sense of guilt? Hell nawl, it doesn't. Noah got what he deserved. The man upstairs don't like ugly and karma was right there to finish his ass off. I've had a couple run-ins with his family, but I'm not worried about any of that. Maybe moving away will lessen the harassment, which I'm pretty much over at this point. I have to talk to my mom and Chade about this, but I will have an answer for you on Monday."

"Sounds like a plan," Wes said, rising to her feet. "I've taken up enough of your time. I'm going to get out of your hair and get back to work.

"Thanks again, Wes," Baylei said as her cell phone rang. Seeing Chade's name had her smiling from ear to ear. "Hey, baby," she said soon as she answered. As she listened to Chade, the smile fell from her face, causing Wes to halt his exit. "Is he alright?" she asked nervously. "Toni should be at work. I will call her." Baylei started scribbling on the notepad on her desk while chewing on her bottom lip.

"Eliminate Jordyn, because she left yesterday to visit Sanji in New York. Toni and I will be there as fast as the plane get us there. Stay calm, Chade. Everything is going to be alright. I love you." Baylei ended the call and looked up at Wes.

"I have to go. Malik was shot and he's in surgery. I have to get ahold of Toni so we can fly out to California. Our flight leaves in two hours."

Baylei explained everything to Wes as she packed up to leave. There was so much she had to organize and she didn't have time to do it at that time. Instead, she grabbed her laptop and stuffed it in her bag along with the project she was working on. Throwing her phone in her purse, she slung it over her shoulder and chucked the garbage from her lunch at Wes.

"Toss that for me please. I don't need any bugs or rodents meeting me at the door when I return. Sorry for rushing out like this, and I'll overnight the project to you as soon as I complete it. I don't know when I'll be back. Just call me and email any work you may have for me."

Baylei was talking a mile a minute moving in circles. Wes, grabbed her by the shoulders and hugged her to his chest. He knew he had to calm her nerves before allowing her to get in her car. Baylei was shaking and Wes could feel the vibrations as he rubbed her back.

"Malik is going to be alright. I need you to get yourself together before you go out there and get into an accident. You're gonna need to be strong for Toni."

"I know. Thank you so much. Malik doesn't bother anyone. Who would shoot him?"

"I'm quite sure Chade will fill you in on all the details once you touch down. Hit me when you get there to let me know you made it. Now get out of here, because you have to go home and pack."

Baylei didn't wait for the elevator to come. She opted to run down the stairs. When she got to her car, her hands shook as she retrieved her phone to call Toni. She dreaded having to tell her friend about Malik, but it had to be done.

"Heyyyyy, Lei. It's not even lunch time and you knocking my line down. You miss me, huh?" Toni laughed. When Baylei didn't join in, all the happiness went out the window. "Lei, what's wrong?"

"Toni, I'm in my car on the way to pick you up. Tell your boss you have an emergency and will be out the rest of the day and you're not sure how long you will be gone."

"What am I doing that for? I can't go on vacation ri—"

"Toni! Do what I asked you to do. I'll be there in fifteen minutes. Be downstairs!" Baylei yelled cutting her friend off. "Malik was shot and we need to get to California. Our flight leaves in less than three hours. We can talk on the way to your house."

"I'll be ready," Toni whispered and hung up.

Toni was downstairs waiting in front of her job when Baylei pulled up and rushed to get in the car. Pulling out in traffic, Toni reached over and turned the volume down on the radio. After buckling her seatbelt, she turned in the seat as best she could, then tossed her purse on the floor.

"Malik getting shot is a surprise to me because he don't fuck with nobody. This shit has Ailani's bitch ass written all over it. Even though Ailani is locked up, the nigga she was creeping around with isn't. I have more than enough money in my account. I'm gon' need you to bail me out because I'm going to jail in Cali-fuckin'-fornia when I get there."

"Toni, we are not going here to get in trouble," Baylei said, trying to reason with her friend. When Toni had her mind made up, there was no changing her mind.

"*You're* not going to get in trouble. Baylei, you know how I am when it comes to bullshit, especially when it involves someone I care about. There's no use trying to debate with me about it because I said what the fuck I said!"

Baylei let Toni's words linger in the air and kept driving. With it being early in the day, there was no traffic. They pulled into Toni's driveway fifteen minutes later. Quickly throwing clothes into a duffle bag, Toni mumbled frustratedly with every step she took. Baylei took that moment to call her mother and tell her about the impromptu trip she was about to take. By the time she got off the phone, Toni was packed and ready to go.

At Baylei's house, she did the same thing as Toni and packed quickly. Anything she forgot would be purchased when she arrived in California.

They made it to the airport with an hour and a half before they were set to board. Baylei had to leave her car at the airport, but she didn't care about the cost. They rushed to security, hoping the lines were too long.

***

Baylei called Chade when they were settled on the plane and he promised to be there to pick them up. He made good on his promise and as soon as they stepped out of the airport into the smoldering heat, Chade was standing outside of his midnight black Denali dressed in a tank top that showed off his muscled arms. The basketball shorts he wore had his python damn near slithering down his thigh. Baylei was intrigued by the sight in St. Thomas, but that shit was a no-go now that she was his fiancée.

"There goes my baby," he sang as if he was Usher Raymond himself as he moved toward Baylei. She ran into his arms and they kissed each other passionately.

The month since they'd seen each other proved how much one missed the other at that moment. Chade's pipe grew with every swap of their tongues and Baylei felt every inch as it rose to the occasion. She broke the kiss and stepped back a bit as she glared at what looked like a tent in the front of his shorts. Slowly bringing her eyes back to Chade's, she cupped his beard, giving it a slight yank.

"Once you get home, I want you to burn them muthafuckas and any others you have like them. This is what we *not* gon' do. You will not be parading around in male thot gear on my watch. All my shit is on full display and I'd hate to bust a bitch upside the head thinking she about to get an ounce of that dick. Stop playing with me, Chade."

The way Baylei bossed up on him only made his joint swell even more. She was sexy as hell when she was angry, and he loved that crazy shit. Licking his lips, he kissed her tenderly and cupped her ass in the palm of his hands.

"You have nothing to worry about. My playa days are over and done with. I know where home is, so you don't have to threaten a nigga about shit. There isn't another bitch walking the face of the earth that can put flame to you, baby. But I will dispose of my 'male thot' gear, as you say, just for you."

The sound of someone clearing their throat brought Chade and Baylei's playful bickering to an end. They forgot all about Toni and felt bad because Malik was laid up in the very hospital where he worked and they knew she was eager to see him. Baylei grabbed her bag while ushering Chade around the car to get inside.

"I'll get the bags. You just pop the trunk, lil thot."

"Baylei, leave that damn man alone so we can go. He's a gentleman and has to do what he knows is right," Toni huffed.

"I'm the gentleman today. You see he's getting in that damn car, right? He should've thought about that before he thought coming out the house in house clothes was going to be alright with me. Now, give me your bag and get yo' ass in the truck."

Toni laughed and did what she was told. When she got in the backseat, Chade turned to her, laughing himself. "Let me find out her ass is low-key crazy and you didn't warn me."

"You stuck with her now because you went out and popped that magical question. Research is very important before taking that step. You let that snappy nappy dugout make you leap before you crawled."

They were laughing hard as hell until the trunk slammed and Baylei got into the car. She sat back like she had a real-life attitude. Neither Chade nor Toni fed into her shenanigans. They rode through the California streets and Baylei took in the sights. According to Chade, the commute was going to take a little over thirty minutes, but that was far from the truth. More like an hour and a half due to traffic.

The laughing, joking, and singing came to a halt the minute they pulled into the parking lot of the hospital. Toni started biting her bottom lip, something she did when she was extremely nervous and Chade peeped it in the rearview mirror. He kept glancing up periodically until he couldn't take it anymore.

"Tone, bro is going to be good. I didn't go into detail about his condition, but I'm here to tell you it wasn't as bad as it looked. He was shot in the side and he had some internal bleeding. They were able to go in and stop that shit. He's heavily medicated. Other than that, he gon' be alright. Malik's health is in the hands of the very people he helps save lives for every day. They're going to make sure he's on his way to a full recovery." Chade reassured her as he parked his truck.

"Why did this happen to him, Chade?" Toni asked with tears streaming down her face.

"We don't know who shot him, but we have an idea."

"It was that nigga that Ailani was fucking with. They are going to pay for this shit," Toni said, getting mad. "All she had to do was walk away when he said it was over between them. I hate a bitch that tries to hold on to someone that no longer wants anything to do with them."

"You are on the right track, and it's nothing you need to worry yourself about. Malik will be glad to see you. Mad at me for arranging for you to see him in this state, but I couldn't follow his orders of not calling you. I'll deal with him even if I have to stop his medicine flow." He laughed, trying to lighten the mood.

"Chade, don't make me beat you. He needs that damn medicine." Toni laughed with his crazy ass. "Come on, I need to see my man. We were just talking about making plans for me to visit. I didn't think he would be in the hospital in order for me to get here faster."

"I'm gon' have to ask this nigga did he plan this shit. What you just said sounds suspect as hell."

"Shut up, Chade!" Baylei yelled, smacking him on his arm.

Getting out of the car, Baylei and Toni walked to the front desk and got passes. Chade still had his from earlier. He led the way to the elevator and to Malik's room. The closer they got to the door, the slower Toni walked. Stopping to wait for her, Baylei held her hand out for support. Toni shook her head no and shooed Baylei away and motioned for her to go ahead.

Ahmad was standing by the door when they entered and he and Chade dapped up.

"How he doing?" Chade asked.

"He's been in and out. That medicine they giving him is potent as hell. His ass be nodding like a muthafucka," Ahmad laughed. "Every thirty minutes he hit that button to get another dose to get right."

"I'll let you in on a secret. Malik is putting on for you niggas because he don't want to talk. That damn morphine is on a timer. It don't come out that damn often." Chade smirked.

"Mind yo' damn business, Mr. Lover Man." Ahmad looked around Chade to see Malik smiling in the bed.

"I've been waiting on their asses to go home. Now you done told them all my business. Remind me to never tell you how certain shit works in the medical field ever again."

Toni walked in with her lips pursed together tightly. Malik turned in the direction of the opened door and shot daggers at Chade. He didn't pay attention to the fact of Baylei being in the room until that precise moment. His scowl turned to a soft smile when he watched Toni walking toward him.

"Hey, baby. What you doing here?" Malik asked.

"Aren't you in the hospital?" He nodded his head yes. "Aren't you *my* man?" Malik nodded again. "So, I'm supposed to be here making sure my man is okay after getting shot, correct?" Malik smiled and nodded his head repeatedly. "Then shut yo' ass up and give me a kiss." Toni bent down and kissed him regardless of his dry lips and tart breath.

Malik moved over in the bed slowly, bringing Toni with him so she could lie in bed with him. He had told Chade not to tell her what happened, but she felt so good in his arms and was glad his boy went against his wishes. They ended the kiss and Malik caressed her thigh as she kissed him all over his face.

"Should we leave and give y'all some privacy?" Samir laughed. "I mean, we can do that."

"My bad. We're done; for now," Malik laughed, never taking his eyes off Toni.

At that moment, the door opened again and in walked Malik Sr. and Cookie. The look on Malik's mother's face, to one that didn't know any better, spoke jealousy silently. She parted her lips to speak, but Malik Sr. halted that shit immediately.

"How are you feeling, son?" Malik Sr. grinned.

"I'm good, Pops. Hey, Ma. Raise the head of my bed and help me sit up, babe," he whispered to Toni. She moved to get up and he stopped her by grasping her thigh. "You don't have to get up. Next to me is where you belong."

Toni helped Malik get comfortable and assumed her position right next to him. Malik was blushing and showed all thirty-two of his teeth. His mother cleared her throat with her arms folded over her chest. Malik took that time to introduce his woman to his parents. After the Ailani fiasco, he knew she was really leery about another woman being close to her son.

"I want y'all to formally meet Toni," Malik said, squeezing her hand. "Baby, this is my father, Malik Sr., and my mother, Jeanette."

"Boy, what's my damn name? You know better than to call me that shit," Cookie snapped.

"My bad, Ma. Baby, that's my mama Cookie. Is that better?"

Cookie ignored Malik and focused her attention on Toni. She was trying to figure her out, but being quiet about it wasn't the way to see where the woman's intentions for her son were. Cookie didn't play when it came to Malik, and everyone who knew her gathered that from the first meeting. There was an intense stare down between the two women and the room was eerily quiet.

"What's your plans with my baby?" Cookie finally asked.

Toni chuckled and positioned herself on the side of the bed. "Nice to meet both of you. Before I answer your question, Miss Cookie—"

"Cookie would be fine."

"Okay, Cookie. Malik is a grown-ass man; no disrespect. Comparing me to the bum he was with previously won't work in your favor because I'm nothing like her. As far as the plans we have for *one another*, our plan is to learn more about each other and see where things go. The feelings between Malik and I are strong, but believe me, we're not rushing to the altar. I can say this though; I'm the woman that's going to stand by his side through thick and thin and make sure he is good in every way imaginable."

Cookie nodded her head in agreement. "Are you with him because of his occupation? I'm quite sure you Googled how much a doctor makes in a year." Cookie was purposely trying to hit several buttons to see how far Toni would be able to hold her composure. Malik didn't need a weak-ass, gold digging, woman by his side.

"Cookie, that's enough!" Malik Sr. roared.

"Nah, let her say what's on her mind, Sir." Toni laughed. "See, Malik's cash flow is the last thing on my mind. I know exactly how much a doctor makes because my salary is just about in the same tax bracket. I have never needed a nigga to do anything for me, *Cookie*. Antonia is capable of taking care of herself quite well. If anything, Malik and I, when the time is right, will invest in many things before we ever go broke. I'm a woman that stands on living below my means. That's why can't nobody speculate about how much money I possess." Toni was semi-angry, but held her own when it came to Malik's overprotective-ass mama. "So you don't have to worry about me using Malik. That's not how I operate. But you would want to figure out how to come for me because I'm not Ailani. Bullying and trying to intimidate me won't work over here. Respecting a man's mother is top priority on my list, *but* the same respect is expected in returned."

The entire time Toni spoke her piece, she never lost eye contact with Cookie. You could hear a pin drop in the room and no one seemed to even take a breath. It was that quiet. Cookie walked toward Toni and Malik Sr. automatically blocked her approach. Finally taking her gaze off Toni, Cookie smiled at her son.

"Now that's how you clap back! She understood the assignment and aced that muthafucka! You got a rider by your side, son. Job well done," Cookie said, clapping her hands as she walked around her husband to hug Toni. Welcome, baby. Thank you for being here for Malik. Sorry for putting you to the test. If you hadn't stepped the fuck up, I was kickin' you out."

Everybody laughed, including Toni. She was glad Cookie stopped with the interrogating because her bantering almost got her ass whooped. Baylei stood beside Chade and gave her friend that look. She knew if things would have gone further, both of them would've been throwing hands with Malik's mother.

"Boy, I told yo' ass about them Chicago women. You done went out and got one that stood up to yo' mama! You in for an adventurous life." Malik Sr. laughed. "What the hell are we gon' do with two Cookies in this damn family?"

"There's only one Cookie. I don't know how many times I have to say that," Cookie said, looking around the room. "All my knuckleheads are here and I wouldn't expect anything less of y'all. Where's Vincent?"

"He's in Chicago. Called and told him what's up. He'll be flying in tomorrow. Sanji will be here sometime tomorrow too," Chade said, filling everybody in as he wrapped his arm around Baylei.

"Mm-hmm. Chade, I know your hoe ass didn't bring a random to a family function." Cookie glanced at Baylei.

"Nah." Chade laughed. "My hoe days are over and so is your memory. Malik told you about the day I proposed to this beautiful jewel right here. This is my fiancée Baylei."

"Hello, Cookie. Nice to meet you," Baylei said, holding her hand out for Cookie to shake.

"We gon' have to toughen you up, chile. You seem too soft and with Chade's past, you gon' need to know how to fight. Those chicks were on his ass like flies on shit."

"She's good just the way she is. Gon' with all that, Cookie." Chade was used to Cookie's wordplay and thought it was funny. But Baylei was meeting her for the first time and he didn't want Cookie to scare her off.

Pointing to Toni, Baylei smirked. "When you see her, you see me. I'm just the mild one of the two. The pretty face fools y'all every time. Don't judge a book by its cover."

"Yeah, buddy. You got your hands full with that one too," Malik Sr. said to Chade. "I'll be looking for the gray hairs to pop out sooner rather than later."

Everyone started getting to know one another for a few hours until Baylei started rubbing on Chade discreetly in what he assumed was a sexual manner while she talked to Cookie and Toni. The way her hand moved up the back of his shirt, running her nails along his spine, had his balls tingling. Chade bent down and whispered in her ear.

"Keep doing that and we gon' have to blow this joint. I ain't had no pussy in forty-five days."

Baylei blushed as she bit her bottom lip. She tried to ignore him because she didn't want anyone to catch on to what Chade was saying to her. It didn't work because her fiancé wouldn't let up about being sex deprived.

"My dick is getting hard and you know what happens when he stands up in these pants I'm wearing. He misses you, baby, and can't wait to massage your sugary walls." Chade licked her ear, sending a shiver down her spine. "Say 'see you later' and let's go home."

"I think it's time for me and Chade to leave. Malik, Toni and I will be back tomorrow," Baylei rushed to say. "Cookie, let me know what day you want me to come over for dinner. I can taste those oxtails already."

"Baylei, go ahead. I'm going to stay here with Malik. I will have to come down and get my bag though," Toni said.

"Don't worry, Tone. I'll bring it back up," Chade chimed in. "Bro, I'll hit you up later to see how you doing."

Chade and Baylei left and Malik Sr. followed. "Hold up, Chade. I want to rap with you."

Chapter 13

"What's up, Big Malik?" Chade asked as they walked down the hall.

Malik Sr. looked out for all of them as they made their way through college. He was the closest thing to a father for Chade and he had nothing but respect for him and Cookie.

"I need to know the details of what happened to Malik."

"We were shooting the shit in front of the crib after you left. Next thing we knew, shots were being fired from a black vehicle. None of the shots were aimed at anybody other than bro. That was a hit."

"I've been seeing shit on the news about the nigga they saw at his house. I got some folks looking into it because I heard his name mentioned in that same segment. Hopefully I find his ass before the fuckin' police." Malik Sr. said as they stepped off the elevator.

Baylei walked ahead so the men could talk amongst themselves. She had heard more than she wanted inside the elevator. Chade knew if Big Malik got his hands on dude, it was lights out for him. He hadn't been watching the news, but he was damn sure going to look up what was being said. Chade had his own sources to stay on the lookout and he was going to use them.

"The shit is going to hit the fan because neither he nor Ailani will get away with bringing trouble to Malik's front door. I'm just glad he's going to be okay to live another day. A lot of people wasn't so lucky out here in these streets." Chade said when they got to the truck. Unlocking the trunk, he grabbed Toni's bag and handed it to Malik Sr.

"Well, you take care and be careful out here."

"I'm going home. I don't do any hanging. Plus, I got my baby here with me and we got some making up to do." Chade smirked, closing the trunk.

"Be safe with that too. Fuck around and make a baby the way you were all over that woman. I love you, son. I'll see you later."

Chade laughed as he got into the truck, where Baylei waited patiently for him to finish his conversation. She looked good in her work attire, but Chade knew she was ready to get out of those clothes and into something more comfortable. Wasting no time pulling out of the lot, he maneuvered his way into traffic and headed towards his home. Baylei ended up falling asleep with her hand clasped in his and that left Chade to think about what Big Malik said about making a baby.

Being someone's father never crossed his mind until that moment. Chade was always known as the man that played the field with many women. A relationship was the last thing he'd ever thought he would hold down after the heartbreak he endured back in the day. It took Baylei to come around and sweep him off his feet. If anyone got a child out of him, it would be his wife.

As Chade pulled into his driveway, he looked over at Baylei and smiled. Removing his hand from the light grip she had on his, he got out and grabbed her bag from the back. He went into the house taking her belongings to his bedroom. Chade started the water in the Jacuzzi tub and added a few bath salts, then made his way back outside to get his fiancée out of the truck.

Baylei was snoring softly. She hadn't moved an inch as he reached over to unbuckle the seatbelt from around her. Cupping her legs with his right arm, Chade placed his left around her back and lifted her out of the truck like a baby. He closed the door with his hip, walking carefully to the house. Baylei stirred, but didn't open her eyes. Chade laughed lowly because she was out of it, which he understood because she woke up very early for work. Stepping into the bedroom after carefully climbing the stairs, Chade kissed Baylei on the lips and placed her on the bed.

"Wake up, Beautiful. We're home," Chade whispered.

Allowing her to sleep a little longer, he left her side, going to the bathroom to check on the water in the tub. After turning the faucet off, he checked the temperature and the water was piping hot. The water should be good until he could wake up the woman that took his heart into the palm of her hands. Chade walked back into the bedroom and started undressing while watching Baylei as if she was a bowl of banana pudding.

Running his hands up her thigh, he unfastened her slacks and slid them slowly over her luscious hips. Baylei stirred a bit, but never woke up. With her love box exposed, he ran a finger up her slit and spread her legs wide. The smell of sweat drifted to his nostrils and it was enough to make his dick swell. There was nothing wrong with the sweet aroma of a day's work, and Chade was about to lick her clean.

With every kiss he planted on her inner thighs, Baylei squirmed. She didn't wake up, so he continued to her creamy middle. Baylei's honey pot was producing nectar even while she slept, which was a bonus for Chade because he needed to quench his thirst. Wrapping his lips around her bud, he sucked on it softly before he went in for the kill. Chade inserted his tongue in her tunnel and a lustful groan escaped his throat.

Baylei's hands went to her breasts, but all she could do was cup them through her blouse. Chade reached up and released the buttons as he continued to lick her lower fleshy lips. She started gyrating her hips, feeding him all the pussy. With her shirt opened, Chade unclasped her bra, which was luckily in the front, and twisted her nipples with his free fingers.

"Fuck!" she moaned. "Right there, baby. Suck harder."

Doing as she asked, Chade cupped his tongue under her clit and flicked it repeatedly before wrapping his lips around it and sucking hard. Baylei still had her eyes closed, but she was still telling him what to do to her. Devouring her pussy, Chade licked her like an ice cream cone with his long tongue. Sticking two fingers into her, he went straight for her g-spot as he kept sucking on her clit.

"Oh shit! Yes, I'm about to cum, baby!" she screamed while thrusting her hips. Baylei let out a tidal wave of cum and Chade caught ever drop. Kissing her kitty one last time, he removed his fingers and licked them clean. "Damn, I need to get to California. That dream felt so damn real."

Chade smiled because it felt good to know she was having wet dreams about them being together. Baylei obviously, envisioned their time together to the point of wishing it was reality. Little did she know, that was just the beginning.

"It was definitely real, Beautiful." The sound of Chade's voice made her eyes pop open. Baylei was so tired, she forgot all about being in California. Take the rest of that shit off and throw that ass on this dick."

Baylei smiled devilishly and Chade was ready for what was to come. Baylei was no joke in the bedroom and it was his for the taking. She hurriedly took off her shirt and bra before assuming the position in front of Chade with the most perfect arch in her back. The sight of her round ass had him salivating as he mended both of them in his hand simultaneously.

"Are you going to stand there admiring my ass or are you gon' give me what the fuck I really came to California for?"

She didn't say nothing but a word to brick Chade's shit up. Sliding the tip up and down he slick middle, Baylei pushed back, trying to force his erection inside, but he wasn't letting her take control. Instead, he gripped her waist and slowly entered her wet cove.

"Yasssss," she moaned, plopping on the mattress.

"Bring yo' ass back here! What the fuck you doing?" Chade barked. "Running from this dick is not acceptable, Beautiful. You 'bout to take all this dick," he said, pulling her back up, and then he pushed her lower back down into the mattress with force.

With Baylei back in position, Chade long-stroked her from behind while his teeth sunk into his bottom lip. The grip she had on his man almost made him scream out like a bitch. He hadn't been up in her kitty in a while but that stroke refreshed his memory on what he was missing out on. With every stroke, her pussy talked to a nigga.

"Yeah, she missed me just as much as I've missed her. That's what I like to hear, talk to me, baby," Chade coaxed as he dug his fingers in Baylei's ass cheeks. Looking down as his dick glided in and out of her wetness, he picked up the pace. Their lower regions were getting very acquainted with one another and the heat was building around them. Chade thrust his hips and Baylei fell flat on the bed once again.

"I see you think we're playing with yo' ass. You gon' take this dick, Beautiful. I thought this is what you came here for," He laughed. "I got something for all that though."

Chade reached over her head and grabbed a pillow. Baylei was confused as to what he was about to do, but she couldn't say anything because her love box was humming loudly and her breathing was labored. When he placed the pillow under her midsection, Baylei's body melted into the fluffy cotton. It was short-lived as Chade forced her back on her knees and pushed her back down, creating the perfect arch.

Guiding his pipe into her water hole, he went to work. Baylei cried out in pleasure, but the way Chade held on to both ends of the pillow, there was no way she could escape the beating he was putting on her lady parts. Dragging the pillow downward, he stood up, bringing her lower half to the edge of the bed. Chade had no mercy on the way he was hitting the bottom of her tunnel.

"Oh my God! I'm about to cum, bae," she moaned loudly.

"That's what the fuck I want you to do. I told you, I didn't come to play. Give me that shit, Beautiful."

With nowhere to run, Baylei didn't have a choice but to take everything Chade was dishing out. Before long, a long stream of cum exploded onto his thighs. That only made him go harder, touching every crevice of her insides. She tried to lower herself onto the bed, but Chade yanked the pillow bringing her right back where he wanted her to be. Digging all in her guts, the sweat on her back glistened and Chade bent down running his tongue over the spot.

"Throw that shit back on me, ma. Arghhh, yo' shit gushy, just how I like it." Chade was fighting the urge to cum because he wanted to make her cum at least two more times.

Spreading his legs apart to balance himself, he held on for dear life to the pillow and plowed into her honey pot while hitting her G-spot repeatedly. Baylei clutched the sheets with her fists balled up as she threw her ass back into him. Chade's toes curled into the carpeted floor and the veins protruded from his forehead as he gritted his teeth.

"Fuck me, baby. This pussy is forever yours. You got all of this, Chade."

The words Baylei was saying had him cheesing like The Joker. She didn't say anything he didn't already know. He staked claim to her shit the first time he got a taste of it.

"I love you, Beautiful. Now wet this dick up."

Chade murdered her twat with no mercy. There was no stopping his nut that was running a marathon to the finish line. "Ahhhhh, yeah. Give it all to me." The way he was yanking the pillow, Baylei couldn't run to save her life. The muscles in her stomach clenched causing her walls to close around his manhood. A few more pumps and they were both cumming in unison. Baylei wet the floor as she squealed in ecstasy. In Chade's mind he pulled out, but in reality, he shot the club up with an extended clip.

Their sex session was one for the books and both of them were tired afterwards. Soaking in the tub led to another round of love-making. After satisfying one another and washing up, Baylei and Chade collapse in the bed and fell asleep. Chade was back up two hours later because Malik getting shot had him restless. He grabbed his phone and threw on his robe before heading downstairs to make a call.

"What up, fam? I ain't heard from you since we were in the Chi last month. Don't tell me you done got yourself in trouble."

"Nah, Juice, I'm all good over here. Malik got shot the other day. Don't panic, he gon' be straight, but you know these streets like the back of your hand and I was wondering if you knew a cat that goes by the name Dex."

"You talking about the nigga that's been all over the news?" Juice asked.

"Yeah, that muthafucka. All that shit got to do with Malik." Chade broke down everything that had transpired and Juice zoned out while listening.

"I know that nigga. He getting paid out in these streets and he's one cocky-ass muthafucka. Me and him don't see eye to eye and he has the nerve to be coming for my people because of the way he runs his business. What you need me to do?"

"I just need an address. His father is going to deal with the nigga personally. He don't want any of us involved," Chade said.

"Oh, that's easy," Juice said, texting Chade the address. "He lives with his baby mama and their twin daughters. I haven't seen his ass around lately, so he's hiding out. The address I gave you will go undetected by the police because it's not in his name."

"How the hell you know about his spot then?"

"Just say, his baby mama fucks with one of my soldiers. She's innocent in all this, so let Malik's dad know they are off limits. Take all that shit up with Dex's punk ass. Tell him to look into the lil light-skinned baddy he was parading around with too."

"You talking about Ailani. That grimy bitch is locked up behind that nigga. They pinned the bricks on her ass because she tried to say the shit was Malik's. It was his surveillance that proved he wasn't involved. She's right where she belongs with her funky ass. Let me get off this phone before my lady wakes up. Thanks, Juice. I'll keep you posted."

"A'ight, bet."

Chade forwarded the address along with the message about the woman and kids to Big Malik and went upstairs to cuddle with Baylei.

Chapter 14

Sitting in the chair beside Malik's hospital bed, Toni was trying to concentrate on the work she had brought along with her. Every few minutes she would look up to make sure Malik wasn't in too much pain. He had a rough night of tossing and turning, but finally settled down when Toni climbed in the bed with him. She eased out about midnight and let the couch bed out so he would be able to sleep comfortably. The doctor said if his fever stayed down, Malik would be able to go home sometime that day.

The ringing of Malik's phone interrupted her flow. She glanced up with a sigh and put her laptop down beside her and rose to answer the device. Malik reached for it on the nightstand before she could get up completely. When he groaned and put the phone down, letting it ring out, it immediately started ringing again.

"Why aren't you answering the phone, babe?" Toni asked.

"It's Ailani's mama again. It's been weeks and I still don't have anything to say to this woman. Far as I'm concerned, she's dead, just like her daughter said she was. I'm through with Ailani, so why would I even open the door to her mama?"

"I think she's trying to tell you something, baby. Call her back and hear her out. That's all I ask," Toni all but pleaded.

Malik picked up his phone and dialed the number back. He put it on speaker so Toni could hear as well. She held his hand sitting next to him on the bed as a woman's voice filled the room.

"Hello."

"May I speak with Alauna please?"

"This is Alauna. I'm so glad you finally called me back, Malik. How long have you known Ailani?" she asked.

"I'd been in a relationship with your daughter for the past four years up until about a month ago."

"Four years! I just learned of you a few weeks ago," Alauna exclaimed. "Did you ever question Ailani about family?"

"I did when we first started dating. She told me her family died in a fire and she was raised in foster care. Ailani was very sad whenever we talked about the tragic events of her life. She told me she came home from school to the fire department dousing out the flames of her childhood home and was told there were still people inside. Me being the man that I am, I put her in therapy to talk out her feelings surrounding that day. It seemed to help her a lot. She was prescribed medication for the anxiety she was experiencing and it worked for her."

"As you can see, Ailani lied to you. Whatever treatment you paid for had nothing to do with the death of her family. I'm living proof of that. Malik, my daughter didn't lose one member of her family until last year when my husband passed away and I couldn't get in touch with her to deliver the news. Let me give you a back story about Ailani," Alauna said, clearing her throat.

"When Ailani was twenty-four, she went out with some friends. She was drugged, raped, and beaten. The person that did these things left her for dead in an alley. Good thing someone found her and called an ambulance. If she wasn't found, I could've lost my daughter that night. Ailani spent a week in the hospital to heal from the attack she endured. When she constantly lashed at staff members as well as myself, they ran a series of psychological tests and diagnosed her as being schizophrenic. Ailani was sent home with medication, but she refused to take them. One day she tried to kill my son while he slept because she said he was the one that hurt her. Brandon was fifteen at the time and was home in bed. Ailani was hallucinating. I had her committed and she was held in a mental institution for three months."

Malik and Toni sat back listening in shock. He had no clue that he was laid up with a crazy woman for the past four years. Toni felt Malik was lucky that he never got on Ailani's bad side. It was probably because he worked so much at the hospital and didn't notice any of the signs. Regardless, he dodged a bullet and she was glad he ended things when he did.

"Ailani was released into my care after passing many psych evaluations," Alauna continued. "I made sure she took her medicine every day and things started looking up for her. Until one day I woke up and Ailani was gone. I searched high and low for her, but Ailani was nowhere to be found. She vanished from Arizona without a trace. That was, until I received a phone call about her arrest."

Malik thought about the story Ailani's mother recited and couldn't do anything besides shake his head. "She didn't give me any vibes of having any type of disorder. Ailani was loving in every way imaginable. The potential of being a great wife was in her. The deception didn't come about until I noticed her mismanaging my money. At that point, I knew the relationship was over because the trust I once had was gone. I'm glad you told me about Ailani's past, but after today, there's no need for you to contact me again. Your daughter is a thing of the past and I've officially closed the door on that part of my life."

Alauna sighed into the phone. "That's where you're wrong. Ailani doesn't do well with rejection. She's no longer in the facility she was locked up in. I don't know all the details, but I went to visit her and was told she wasn't there. She was taken to the hospital after being beaten and she hasn't returned. If my daughter is out and about, she's going to come for you, Malik. I want you to be careful. Think long and hard about blocking me. It wouldn't be wise. I'm going to keep you updated on any new information I receive, so keep your phone close."

"Your daughter can come for him if she likes," Toni let her presence be known. "She's going to wish she would've stayed far away from Malik because I owe her an ass whooping for old and new. I hope you have a hefty insurance policy in place. You're going to need it."

"Truthfully speaking, that's exactly what I'm afraid of. Ailani nine times out of ten is off her meds. The look in her eyes told me such when I visited her. She's not herself right now. When she shows her face, she won't be the same woman you've dealt with in the past, Malik. I just want you to be careful."

"Thanks for giving me a heads up. I wish you and your daughter the best. If she pops up, I'll be sure to give you a call; after I call the police. My career is important to me and taking care of Ailani on some street shit isn't what I do."

"Well, I can live without my career. The bitch gon' end up in a ditch fuckin' with me. I won't have no type of mercy on her ass. Mark my words." Toni was fuming. Malik could go the high road with the crazy bitch, but she wasn't about to play with her crazy ass. "You have a nice day, Alauna. Malik will keep in touch." Toni reached over and ended the call. Malik stared at her for a few seconds then laughed out loud.

"Yo' ass is gangsta as fuck. Why did you tell that woman you would kill her daughter?"

"What, you wanted me to lie? I don't do that type of shit. My career doesn't define who I am. I may be a paralegal, but I was born and raised on the Southside of Chicago. I will do any and everything to protect myself. I know the law. Making that shit look like a self-defense case will be breezy fuckin' with me. I'm sure if Ailani comes with the bullshit, I will be first on her list because I got her man."

"Ailani isn't going to do nothing to anyone. We have nothing to worry about." Malik tried to reassure Toni, but she wasn't falling for what he said.

"Did you hear what her mama said? I believed every word and the bitch is crazy. You can downplay that shit, but I'm not. Like Alauna said, she's not the person you were laid up with for four years. Open your eyes, Malik."

Malik pulled Toni down next to him and kissed her tenderly on the lips.

There was a light knock on the door and the doctor entered with a smile on his face. Toni stood from the bed to make room for the doctor to do whatever he needed with Malik.

"Dr. Daniels, you are healing very well and I think you are ready to go home. I have your discharge papers here. The only thing you will have to do is go down to the pharmacy and pick up your prescriptions for pain. I don't have to tell you how to keep your wound clean, but it's in your paperwork in case you've forgotten." The doctor laughed.

"Jerry, I know how to care for myself. Hell, I could've stitched myself up, but you guys wouldn't let me do it."

Malik and his colleague laughed about the situation, letting Toni know they had a great relationship at work. Everyone that came into the room was glad Malik was doing well after being shot. He was loved and appreciated at Cedars Sinai, which meant he was one hell of a doctor.

"Well, bud, you are not to report back to work for a month. We want what's best for you and make sure you're healed in and out." Malik opened his mouth to speak, but Jerry silenced him. "It's not up for debate. You are officially back on vacation."

Jerry didn't wait around to hear what Malik had to say. He left the room faster than he entered. Malik looked as if he was pissed and Toni knew it was because he was forced to stay home.

"Fix your face. You need to be home to heal properly. There's no way you can help anyone in this hospital if you're not a hundred percent yourself. Now is the time for you to concentrate on Dr. Daniels the way you do your patients. If the shoe was on the other foot, you would suggest the same for someone else. Now, tell me I'm wrong."

"You're right. I just don't believe I need to be off that amount of time."

"I'm not trying to hear that. You could've stopped at 'you're right' to be honest," Toni laughed. "Let me call Baylei to come get us so we can blow this joint. I'm tired of being in this sterile box of a room."

After making the call to Baylei, Toni got Malik's clothes together and assisted him with his shower. He drew the line with her helping him get dressed, so she took that time to pack her things up. She couldn't wait to get to his home so she could love on him properly. Toni promised herself not to put the kitty on him too much, but she needed to feel him inside her.

Chapter 15

Since being in protective custody, Ailani had been closed off in the apartment by herself, but with an officer outside to make sure she didn't leave the premises. Being cooped up inside was starting to take a toll on her. Actually, it had nothing to do with her being stuck indoors, but a lot to do with her body not receive the medication it required. The voice in her head had been trying to get her to run all morning. Ailani was tired of going back and forth with her because she knew running would lead to more trouble.

"You need to get us the hell out her, Ailani! I need sunlight to live. Being in this small-ass apartment is making me claustrophobic."

"Christine, why are you even here right now? You're always trying to make me do things I'm not proud of in the end. Just go away!" Ailani yelled, pounding the side of her head.

"That's not going to happen this time." Christine laughed. "That damn medicine isn't going to save you this time. You should've told the pigs you were on medication and you needed it to survive out here in this dreadful world. In my Tony Montana voice, the world is mine."

The evil laugh inside Ailani's head scared her to no end. Even if she received a dose of her medication, it wouldn't make the evil person that lived within her go away. She'd been off the meds too long. Ailani experienced her first episode right before meeting Malik, and it didn't end well for the guy she was seeing. The events of that day played back in her mind and made her cringe.

Ailani met Nate as soon as she stepped foot on California soil. He was a fine chocolate brother. Nate literally ran into Ailani when while she rushed down the street without a destination in mind. She was hungry and hoped like hell she would be able to luck up on a meal. Not watching where she was going, she ran into something that felt like a brick wall. Falling on the ground with a thud, Ailani hit her head on the base of a fire hydrant and was dazed for a few minutes.

"I'm so sorry. Are you okay?" he asked, bending down to check the back of her head.

Ailani couldn't formulate a word, so she nodded her head yes, even though three of him danced before her eyes. Reaching his hand out to help her up, Ailani accepted his help with a slight smile. Finding her voice, she got lost in the stranger's eyes. "No, I'm sorry. I should've been watching where I was going. Thanks for helping me up," she said, trying to get past his muscular body.

"Wait a minute. Don't run off so fast. How about I make up for this little mishap and buy you dinner?"

"No, that's alright. I don't go off with strangers, but thanks for the offer."

"I'm Nate, and I want to take you to get something to eat. Nothing more, nothing less," he said, looking around. "We can actually go right across the street to the steakhouse. I promise, all I want is to grab something to eat."

Ailani's stomach growled loudly at that moment, causing Nate to grab her hand leading her to the restaurant. Fighting him on his offer was a thing of the past because she was finally getting what she hoped for.

Once they were seated, Ailani told him her name and the fact that she was new to California. She gave him a made-up sob story about running scared from an abusive boyfriend. Nate felt sorry for her and offered to put her up in a hotel room for a month. Ailani was grateful for his generosity.

Nate made good on his word and got a room for Ailani and left. A few days later, Ailani was sleeping in bed when Nate came in to check on her. Christine was the one that woke up, which wasn't good for Nate. She ended up stabbing him with a piece of a lamp she had broken. After stealing his money out of his pockets, she left out the back of the hotel without being seen.

Ailani knew if she left, Christine was going right after Malik. She didn't want that to happen. Looking out the window, Ailani could see the officer sitting in his patrol car nodding off.

"The time is now. Look at his fat ass falling asleep." Christine laughed. "You can leave this bitch and he won't know you're gone. Get yo' ass up and let's roll!"

"No! I'm in enough trouble."

"Nough, said." Ailani's vision blurred and she went into a deep sleep. "I don't have time to be sitting in this bitch arguing with your sex-craved ass. There's shit that needs to be handle and yo' ass in here whining."

Christine took over Ailani's body and soul as she put on the ugly ass jail appointed sneakers that sat by the sofa. She looked out the window again before making her move. Closing the door, she checked both ways down the hall before racing for the stairwell. Christine flew out of the building and dashed across the street. She spotted a young girl walking down the street and jogged to catch up with her. When the girl hit the key fob and the lights to a Toyota Camry flashed, Christine became happier than a sissy in a roomful of dicks.

Acting as if she had a gun, Christine pointed her finger in the girl's back. "Don't scream. Give up the fucking keys and walk with me to the passenger side of the car."

"Please don't hurt me," the girl cried. "I have money."

"Move!" Christine gritted through her teeth as she guided her to the other side of the car.

Once she had the girl inside, Christine ran to the other side and got into the driver's seat. Easing into traffic, she rode into the daylight as if she didn't just get ghost on LAPD.

Meanwhile, Detective Lemon got out of his unmarked car to check on Ailani. He first stopped at the car of the undercover officer that was left to watch the building. When he walked up, he could've sworn Pierre was sleeping, but he was proved wrong when he got to the driver side window.

"How's everything going?" Detective Lemon asked.

"It's been quiet. She was looking out the window a while ago so that only means she's getting antsy. Any luck on Hinton?"

"Nah. None of the addresses in the database panned out. His ass is way under the radar right now. I put a hold on all visits to Miss

Denton at the jail as of today. I should've done that shit yesterday because her mother went up there to see her and was told she was taken to the hospital. I made sure everyone knew not to give out information to anyone. That's the only way we would be able to keep her safe."

"Hopefully, that little mishap won't put a damper in your plans. We need her to testify once we get Dex in custody."

"I think we'll be good. I'm going up to make sure she has everything she needs. I'll be back."

Detective Lemon walked into the building and took the elevator up to the unit he had Ailani in. He knocked on the door out of respect, but she didn't acknowledge it. Without waiting, he inserted the key and let himself inside. It was deathly quiet, other than the sound of the television that was tuned in on *The Young and the Restless*. Detective Lemon removed his gun from his holster because something felt off. As he looked around with every step he took, he entered the bedroom. It, too, was empty. After checking closets, the bathroom, and under the bed, he came to the conclusion that his perp was gone.

"Son of a bitch!" he said heading for the door.

He took the stairs fast as he could but it was no use. He knew Ailani had been gone for a while and he had no clue where she was. Approaching Pierre's car with a sinister snarl, Detective Lemon damn near snatched him through the window by his collar. Pierre looked scared because he had no clue what was going on, but he soon found out.

"Your ass was sleeping on the job and let her get away, you fat fuck! You had one job! One fucking job, and you failed!" Spit flew from Detective Lemon's mouth and landed on Pierre's nose. "You fucked up, Pierre. You fucked up!" he said, pushing him back into the car and walked away.

As the detective hopped back in his car, he called his superintendent and explained what happened. An APB was put out for Ailani and hopefully they would get a hit on her whereabouts before she got too far away.

Chapter 16

Three days had passed since Malik was released from the hospital and he and Toni was sitting back watching TV. She had him watching a Lifetime movie about a woman suspecting her husband of having an affair. She hired a private investigator to prove her husband's infidelity. Come to find out, the PI was a man that was stalking another woman seven months prior and she was hit by a car and died. Now he was smitten by Lizza, the lady that went in for his help.

"Man, that nigga about to make her life a living hell. That's the same man that chased that woman in the street at the beginning. Whew, baby, this about to be a good one."

"Toni, I can't believe you got me watching this bullshit. Dude is about to be on the same stalker shit he was on with ole girl in Chicago. How about we watch an action movie or something?" Malik asked.

"No. I want to see what Ethan gon' do to turn this couple's life upside down," Toni shot back. "Look how he just obtained her address! Yeah, he's crazy for real!"

At that moment, the doorbell rang, and Malik took that opportunity to escape watching the psychotic show that Toni was forcing him to watch. Reaching the door, he peeked through the blinds and saw Chade, Baylei, Sanji, and Jordyn standing on the porch.

"Open the door, nigga!" Chade yelled.

Malik smiled as he unlocked the door and stepped back so they could enter. He hadn't seen them since the day he got home. Now, they wanted to turn up because they had food and drinks in stow. Baylei and Jordyn went straight to the kitchen to start cooking and the guys went to the bar.

"Where is my best friend?" Jordyn asked.

"I'm right here! Y'all could've called before coming to this bitch!" Toni said entering the kitchen. "Interrupting my Lifetime movie." She hugged both of her friends then started looking in the bags. Who about to cook all this shit?"

"Chade and Sanji is cooking the meat on the grill, and we gon' cook the sides," Baylei said.

"When the hell you start speaking French? I didn't sign up to be Betty Crocker today."

"Toni, don't start. You probably ain't cooked for the man since you've been here, but you about to start."

"See that's where you wrong. I've slaved in the kitchen for mine. His ass was down up until today and you know damn well I'm not going a day without eating."

"Anyway, help me clean this meat so we can season it." Jordyn was washing her hands while laughing at her two friends when Sanji walked behind her, kissing on her neck. He had her giggling like a schoolgirl as she pushed back on the bulge in his pants.

"Aht, aht. Get yo' freaky ass out of here, Sanji. Y'all should've did all that shit before coming over here. The only folks having relations in this house is me and mine," Toni chastised, pushing Sanji towards the kitchen entryway.

"You trippin' woman. Aye, Malik. Toni needs some act right. I think you need to wrap your wound and give her a few long strokes because she agitated like a muthafucka!" Sanji yelled as he left the women in the kitchen.

"Get off my, baby. She's going to be alright. I'm gon' handle that in due time."

The sound of the men laughing could be heard as the jokes kept going on about Toni. Baylei quietly emptied the bags as she contemplated telling her friends about her new job opportunity. Handing the steaks and sausages to Toni, she then gave Jordyn the baked beans and spaghetti so she could get them started.

"I got a new position at work," Baylei finally got the nerve to say. "I sent Wes an email before coming here telling him I accept his offer."

"Congratulations, Lei," Jordyn cheered. "You deserve that shit. I'm so proud of you."

"I guess that means you get a bigger office and a substantial pay raise, huh?" Toni smirked.

"Yeah, all of that. I'm also relocating. The position is here in California."

Toni paused and the atmosphere change drastically. "How long has your sneaky ass been holding on to this information?"

"I found out the day I got the call about Malik. I wasn't trying to hide anything. I had to talk to my mama about it, then I told Chade the other day. Toni, you know good and damn well you've been taking care of Malik and we haven't talked much. That's the reason I'm here now trying to spend time with your water head ass."

"Mm-hmm. Tell me anything. When is your almost married ass talking about moving?"

"Once I leave here, I'll be going back home to pack up. Chade is going to arranging all the moving, but he insists I give everything away to someone in need. He says all I need to bring back is myself."

"Fuck that! You got some dope shit. I'm going through everything before you give away. You better take your clothes though."

"I'm not leaving my clothes; especially my shoes." Baylei laughed.

The ladies finished seasoning the food, taking it out to the guys who already had the grill nice and hot. The sides were almost ready when the doorbell rang for the second time that day. Toni beat Malik to the door and on the other side stood Vincent, Samir, and his wife Selena. The whole crew was in attendance except Ahmad.

"Hey, y'all. I love how everybody was invited to my crib without my knowledge." Malik smiled. "I wouldn't have it any other way. Come on in. Everybody's out back. Selena, the ladies are in the kitchen."

Toni caught the roll of Selena's eyes and waved her hand at her stuck-up ass. She went back to the kitchen with a mean scowl on her face. Baylei walked to the entryway to see what had her friend looking sour. When she locked eyes with Selena, she motioned for her to join them. Selena smacked her lips and walked across the room and out of the patio door.

"I don't know what's wrong with her ass," Toni quipped. "I don't recall any one of us saying or doing anything that would warrant her to have a chip on her shoulder. As a matter of fact, let me go ask the bitch what her problem is." Toni headed for the backyard and Baylei grabbed her just in time by the arm.

"Nope. Leave that shit where it's at. We're not about to feed into her nonsense. It doesn't matter what her problem is. She has to deal with that all by her lonesome. You will end up beating the hell out of that woman."

Toni sat at the table while Baylei and Jordyn put the finishing touch on the coleslaw and potato salad. Toni gathered up the plates, napkins, and the utensils to take outside. Baylei knew what she was on, but there was no way she could prolong the tongue lashing that was destined to happen. Placing the cold dishes in the fridge, Baylei turned the fire off under the corn on the cob and grabbed the hot dog and hamburger buns to take outside.

"Come here with yo' fine ass," Chade called out to Baylei. He watched her walk across the patio after sitting the bread on the table. The sea green maxi dress she wore hugged her hips nicely, and he couldn't wait to peel it off her later. Gathering her in his arms, Chade lowered his head and captured her lips between his teeth. "I love the fuck out of you, Beautiful," he said, pecking her lips.

"What the fuck is your problem, Selena?" Toni's voice boomed out of nowhere. "You've had your head up your ass since we were introduced to your snobby ass in St. Thomas. Today's the day to get to the bottom of your bullshit."

"Whoa! What the hell just happened?" Malik asked.

"I'm tired of her turning her nose up whenever one of us is in her presence. The only thing Baylei did was walk out here and over to her man and Selena sitting over there as if somebody put shit on the tip of her big-ass snout! I want to know what the problem is so we can rectify the shit."

"There's nothing wrong with me. I don't give a damn about none of y'all, to be honest." Selena crossed her legs and took a sip from the wine cooler she was nursing. You and your friends are the reason Ahmad ain't here today. When's the last time any of y'all heard from him, huh? I bet money not one of y'all can answer that question."

"Selena, Ahmad isn't here because he had some work he needed to finish. He will definitely be here before the night is over. And to bust your bubble, I talk to my boy every muthafuckin' day. Now, I'm with Toni, what's really going on with you?" Chade asked as he stared daggers at her. The whole time, Samir sat back smoking a blunt without uttering a sound.

"Humph, whatever," was all Selena could come up with to say.

"Whatever my ass! Samir, you need to check ya girl 'cause she outta pocket. I don't know if it's because she longs for the attention that's being given to me and my girls or what, but you need to do better at your home front," Toni snapped. Malik pulled Toni to her feet and hugged her around the waist.

"Calm that shit down, bae. Ignore Selena."

"Nah, how about fuck Selena. She's going to learn to respect us or stay her ass at home. Plain and simple."

"It has nothing to do with respect. Since y'all been around, nothing good has happened within the circle that was in place before y'all showed up. Ahmad is no longer with the woman he was supposed to spend the rest of his life with, because of you. Malik got shot, because of you. My marriage is in shamble, because of y'all."

Samir slammed his bottle of beer on the table and glared at Selena with fire in his eyes. She'd taken shit too far with putting their business out in the open for all his boys to hear. No one knew the turmoil his marriage was in until Selena opened her mouth.

"You talk too fuckin' much, and no one is at fault for the way my marriage is today but us. We deal with that shit in private and not out in public. If you had anything to say to me, we could've addressed that shit back at the house. You can't go blaming these women for none of the shit that took place because they didn't have anything to do with how things went down." Samir's face was beet red and he was beyond mad.

"The shit that happened with Ahmad was all on Chasity. If Toni hadn't told him what was up, he would be married to a bitch that didn't love him and miserable as fuck. Let's not forget that you were the one that brought Ailani's infidelity to my attention. So, if you want to blame that on anyone, blame yourself. But that situation was all on Ailani!"

"Aye, y'all go in the house and hash that shit out," Malik said calmly.

"That won't be necessary. I'll just leave."

Selena got up, snatched her purse from the table, and walked out. Samir sat back down and relit his blunt without attempting to go after his wife. Everybody stood around quietly, but all eyes were on him. He reached over and turned the speaker up and let The Lox "Fuck You" blare through the air. Samir put emphasis on the words "fuck you" and that had the guys walking over to cop seats at the table. Malik turned the volume down and looked his homie in the eyes.

"Talk to us, fam. What's really going on?" he asked with his hands folded on top of the table.

"Fuck her, man. I'm not about to get into what's going on in my household. She'll be a'ight once I get back to the crib. It's nothing for y'all to worry about. That's the type of shit that happens when you say 'I do'. I'm sorry y'all had to witness that shit, but I'm tired of her blaming everything on y'all ladies," Samir said, taking a puff from his wood.

"You know she's tight with Chasity and because she's living a miserable life, she wants to bring that same energy to other people. On behalf of my wife, I apologize to you ladies. Y'all haven't done anything except bring joy to the lives of my brothers. I'm with that shit and I thank y'all, for real. I've ruined the vibe so I'm gon' head out so y'all can enjoy the rest of the night."

"You don't have to leave, man," Sanji said, clutching Samir's arm so he couldn't get up.

"Nah, I'm good. I have too much on my mind right now and I don't want to bring the vibe down more than I already have. I'll get up with y'all later. Enjoy the rest of the night."

"Am I missing something here?" Sanji asked in confusion. "What the hell was that about?"

"We have no idea," Chade replied shaking his head. "I didn't know she was still communicating with Chasity, to be honest."

"Birds of a feather," Toni muttered. "I can just imagine what's going on in their marriage. Selena is holding a grudge about something that had nothing to do with her. I didn't break up that union. Her thot-ass friend did."

"Ahmad isn't here to speak on that situation, so we won't dwell on it. We're here to have fun. Turn the music back up and let's eat. I'm hungry as hell."

Malik walked to the grill, flipping the meat. Samir and Selena's issues were something he wasn't going to feed into because he had enough of his own shit to deal with. Malik didn't need to add more to his plate. All he wanted to do was enjoy his friends and the woman that had been standing by his side through it all.

Meesha

Chapter 17

Driving away from Malik's house, Selena was livid as she sped through the California streets. No one knew how bad she wanted to knock Toni in her smart-ass mouth. From the moment Chade invited those bitches to party with them in St. Thomas, Selena didn't have any plans of getting to know them. When everything went down with Ahmad and Chasity, Selena tried her best to stay away at all costs.

Chasity and Selena became close relatively fast and stayed that way even after the events on her wedding day. Selena tried her best to uplift Chasity every day because she often went in and out of depression. What she did was wrong and Selena knew that, but Ahmad didn't have to embarrass her the way he did.

Selena thought about going home, but she didn't want to deal with Samir at the moment. The way he spoke to her at Malik's house wasn't nothing short of what he'd been doing since I was six months pregnant. Samir wasn't the doting husband he wanted everyone to believe he was. Selena caught him in one too many lies and he refused to come out with the truth. She'd been sitting around acting the part, but she let out some of the shit that was on her mind that day.

After pulling along the curb of the park, Selena exited her car and went straight for the swing set and took a seat. She found herself going to that place whenever she needed to clear her mind and she didn't like the way her life took a drastic turn. She and Samir were happily in love for years, then shit shifted and she felt the exact moment it went left.

The late nights, the unanswered calls, and the standoffish way Samir walked around their four-bedroom home without saying a word to Selena only caused her to turn into a spy. The saying "seek and you shall find" is the honest to God truth because what was found shattered Selena's soul. She didn't come right out with her findings but it didn't matter. Samir was taking that shit to his grave.

Selena sat for an hour before she got back in her car, driving aimlessly to avoid being alone in the house. Her stomach growled and she decided to sit down and eat since she left before getting anything at Malik's. Selena had a taste for some wings and headed into the direction of the nearest Hooters. Sitting at a red light, she strained her eyes at a woman that walked in front of her car. It looked like Ailani, but she wasn't sure. She lowered the window and shouted out.

"Ailani! Ailaniiiiii!"

Instead of stopping, she looked over her shoulder erratically and took off running down the street before ducking around the corner out of sight. Samir told Selena what happened with Malik and she was under the impression that Ailani was in jail. The way she took off, she had probably escaped. Putting the encounter in the back of her mind, Selena pulled into the parking lot of Hooters and prepared to get her grub on.

After being seated, Selena sat strolling her social media as she waited for the Buffalo wings the waitress placed for her. She laughed at all the idiots that were damn near killing themselves doing the latest trend called "The Crate Challenge". She couldn't believe they were doing something so dangerous. As another video loaded, her phone rang with a Facetime call from Samir. She politely declined the call, which had become a frequent thing for her to do, and continued laughing at her phone.

When her food and strawberry lemonade were placed before her, Selena wasted no time digging in. The wings were good and she was barely breathing as she demolished them. Her phone chimed with back-to-back texts, but Selena kept eating without reading them. Selena would deal with Samir on her time; not his.

About thirty minutes later, Selena had her card back and left a hefty tip. She sat at the table to check the messages from Samir. Nine times out of ten, he was probably acting like he was her daddy and she was out past curfew.

Hubby: So, you sending me to voicemail now?

Hubby: You have thirty minutes to get home before you piss me off.

The thirty minutes he'd spoken of had long since passed and Selena didn't give a fuck. Had he checked the way he spoke to her earlier, she would've been home. Now he would have to wait until she arrived and even then, she wasn't about to feed into his nonsense.

Selena took her time getting to the residence she shared with her husband. When she pulled into the driveway, the front door swung open and there stood Samir. Exiting her car, Selena locked the doors and walked up the stairs and right past her husband.

"You just gon' walk in here like I haven't been calling and texting you?"

Selena sat her purse on the sofa and turned to her husband with a smirk on her face. "That shit doesn't feel good, huh? Now you know how I feel when you leave me on read and refuse to answer when you're out. I didn't do that shit purposely, but I wasn't ready to talk after what you pulled in front of your friends. You have your nerve, Samir."

"No, you're the one that wanted to run your mouth in front of an audience. I didn't give a damn about you voicing your thoughts, but bringing our marriage out in the open was a no go. Why would you do that?"

"You're ashamed of your infidelities, Samir? You were running around fuckin' these bitches with no shame! Why not let your *boys* in your shit?" Selena laughed. "Let me find out you scared of being judged. Muthafucka, I'm ashamed to still be in this damn house with you, let alone pretending I'm a happy-ass wife." Selena's laughter turned to hurt in a millisecond.

"I told you I didn't sleep with neither one of them women! Why won't you believe me, Selena?"

"I don't believe you because you're lying! I know this for a fact," she cried, walking to her purse. Searching for her phone, Selena went to her social media inbox and pulled up a message that was sent to her months prior. "Isn't this you, Samir? The lies stop today!" she asked, showing him the photo.

There was no way he could deny that it wasn't him in the picture because he had on an outfit Selena gifted him for the very trip Samir claimed he was going on for business. He was palming the woman's kitty from behind on Miami Beach. The nigga was all smiles and the hoe couldn't wait to slide in Selena's inbox to let it be known what her husband was doing instead of working.

"That's an innocent photo, Selena. I met her there, and—" Selena slapped the next words down his throat.

"That bitch works with you, Samir! Don't fuckin' play with me! You can have all this shit. I'm done playing the fool. You're free to do whatever the fuck you choose, but I won't stand around as if I'm oblivious about it. I've done everything I'm supposed to do as your wife. Cook, clean, fuck, suck, and keep a smile on your face; so I thought. After tonight, you no longer have to worry about me putting your needs first. It's time for Selena to put self on the forefront." Selena headed up the stairs quickly until Samir's words halted her steps.

"If you're thinking about leaving, you better think again. We will work this out, Selena. I stand on what I said. There's nothing going on between me and that woman!"

"Tell that shit to someone that believes it. Kiss my ass, Samir."

Selena went upstairs, packed a bag, and was out of the house in fifteen minutes. Samir didn't try to stop her and that was wise of him because she was ready to snatch his head off. The anger she'd been carrying around for months; only a fraction came out that night. She had so much more to get off her chest. It wasn't worth the fight. Samir Jamison could kiss her natural ass.

Chapter 18

"Daddy! Deliya hit me," Dex's daughter Delilah wailed from the playroom.

Dex jumped to his feet to see what the war between his daughters were about that day. Most of the time they were best of friends, but on occasion, they were going at one another's throats. Being identical twins could be a blessing and a curse at times. Delilah was sitting in the middle of the floor crying her little heart out while Deliya stood over her with a finger in her face.

"Stop being a crybaby. Always telling on somebody. We tough and don't cry about everything. You know what daddy said; suck it up, little grasshopper."

"Daddy said if somebody hit us, knock they ass out too." Delilah stood up and Dex stormed in the room to break up the commotion.

"Whoa! What's going on in here and why are you in here cussin', Lilah?" Delilah's chin dropped to her chest, causing Dex to drop to his knees so he was eye level with her. Lifting her chin as tears fell, he wiped them away. "When I told you that, it didn't mean you go hard at your sister. Deliya, come here."

His oldest daughter by two minutes walked over with a smile on her face. "Yes, Daddy?"

"Ain't nothing funny. Keep your hands to yourself and stop bullying your sister. We've talked about this before and you're still at it. Now, get up there and take a nap."

"She touched my doll and I told her not to do it. She didn't listen, so I had to show her I wasn't playing," Deliya pouted.

"And you're not listening right now. What do you think is going to happen to you in three seconds if you don't get your little tail in that bed?"

Deliya opened her mouth to say something else and Dex gave her the look. Yeah, the one Grandma used to give the kids before she had them going outside for the switch; that look. The twins changed roles because Deliya was crying a river while her twin sister laughed silently while sticking her tongue out. Dex saw the look on his oldest daughter's face and caught Delilah in the act.

"Yep, get yo' ass up there too. I don't want to hear a peep out of either one of you or y'all will not like the daddy I will be forced to become. Now behave, and I love both of y'all."

Dex stood waiting for them to say they loved him too, but at that time, there was no love for his ass. He laughed and turned off the light before stepping out of the girls' room. With moves to make, he went to his room and gathered his phone, wallet, and his pistol. As he walked toward the door, he saw Melissa in the kitchen dancing to music as she prepped the food for dinner. The way her hips swayed had him bricking up, but he had to shake the vision from his head.

"I'm heading out," Dex called over his shoulder.

"What you telling me for?" Melissa shot back. "You ain't been announcing your comings and goings, so don't start today."

As soon as Dex left the house, Melissa's phone rang. She smiled hard because it was her boo Jarrod, better known as J-Rock in the streets. "Hey you."

"Aye, check it out. There's about to be somebody pulling up to yo' crib. Is that nigga there?"

"No, he just left a few minutes ago. Who the hell coming here, Jarrod?"

"Just let them in and answer all of their questions. I'll be through shortly, so pack you and the girls a few bags because you're coming with me until further notice."

With that being all he had to say, J-Rock hung up and the doorbell rang. Melissa placed her phone on the counter and hesitantly walked toward the door. Not answering the door fast enough for whomever was on the other side, loud knocks vibrated off the wall, causing her to scream out. Melissa rushed back to the kitchen as the banging continued and call J-Rock.

"What's up, Lissa?"

"Someone's trying to knock the front door off the hinges. I'm scared, Jarrod," Melissa cried.

"Hold on a second." The phone went silent and the knocking suddenly stopped. Jerrod came back on the line as Melissa grabbed a huge butcher knife from the block. "Babe, you're still there?"

"Yes. Why would you put me on hold at a time like this?"

"Go open the door, Lissa. I promise they won't hurt you. I'm going to stay on the phone until you open the door. I'm on my way right now."

Melissa walked slowly to the door and turned the locks. It was pushed open in a matter of seconds, forcing her to back up cautiously with the knife clutched in her fist. The big burly dude was intimidating as hell. The grim look on his face spoke to Melissa without words. In her mind, he was there to kill her. If they came in contact under different circumstances, his old ass could've been a prime candidate for being her Sugar Daddy. But as for now, Melissa stood frozen in place with the phone plastered to her ear, scared senseless.

"Lissa! What's going on?" J-Rock's voice snapped her out of the daze she was in.

"Um, I think I'm about to die."

The burly dude stepped further into her home and Melissa stepped back with every movement of his legs. A second person entered and she let out a sigh of relief when she recognized him.

"I think I'm going to be okay; Juice is here too."

"I told your scary ass nothing was going to happen to you. Be honest with them, Lissa. I'll see you in ten."

Melissa went to the living room and sat in the chair on the far side of the room. Juice raced up the stairs with his gun drawn while the older guy checked the lower half of the house the in the same manner. Both men came back to the room she was seated in and stood silently. Juice broke the silence and Melissa listen intently.

"I'm sorry to barge in on you like this, ma, but I'm quite sure you know what ya baby daddy been up to as of late."

"I don't know nothing, Juice. You of all people know there's nothing going on between Dex and I other than the twins," Melissa rushed to say.

"The shit is all over the news. It can't be missed. That's neither here nor there though. The nigga fucked up when he shot this man's son and could've ended his life. Where is he?" Juice asked, folding his arms over his chest.

"I don't know where he is, Juice. He left a couple minutes before y'all knocked on the door. I'm not trying to be mixed up in anything Dex has going on. I have to think about my kids before anything. I'll try my best to help any way I can."

The older guy stepped forward, but his demeanor softened a tad bit. "I need his number, where he hangs out, and anything else you can provide. Right now isn't the time for you to lie for him. The nigga is going to take his last breath very soon. There's no getting around that."

Melissa chewed on her bottom lip and tears threatened to fall from her eyes. She and Dex weren't in an intimate relationship, but he was a damn good father and her girls needed and loved the hell out of him. Melissa honestly didn't know Dex was even mentioned on the news and she was fucked up about him not mentioning he was wanted. That explained why he hadn't been out of the house, claiming he wanted to spend more time with the girls. That gave her time to spend with Jarrod without paying for a sitter.

"He was fucking around with a chick named Ailani. Do you know anything about her?" the older guy asked.

"I don't question him about what he's doing once he walks out of this house. Whatever he did with that woman is between the two of them. Dex drives a cobalt blue BMW. The license plate number is DEX9080. He has many traps, but he frequents the one on Hepburn Avenue and Martin Luther King Jr. Boulevard in Crenshaw. His mother lives not too far away on Cherrywood Avenue."

Melissa gave them all she knew as the doorbell rang. Juice took the liberty of getting the door and J-Rock entered looking fine as hell, licking his lips. His six-foot frame along with his muscular build made her lady parts do a happy dance in spite of her circumstances. He wore a black tank with a pair of denim shorts with white Jordans. The black fitted he had on was turned backwards, giving

Melissa a full view of his facial features. Melissa damn near ran to him and threw her arms around his neck.

J-Rock hugged her tightly and kissed the top of her head. "Y'all get the information needed?" he asked without releasing Melissa.

"Yeah, baby girl didn't hold back. Get her and the kids out of here. Since I know where the nigga lay his head, I'm not going to chase this fool. All I need him to do is keep thinking shit is sweet and bring his ass home. The info she gave was good, but I won't go looking for him."

J-Rock patted Melissa on the back. "Go pack quickly so we can get out of here."

Melissa moved out of his embrace and walked slowly toward the stairs. She looked back and decided not to say anything further. Dex had written a check his ass wouldn't be able to cash. She had to get her babies far, far away from him and the bullshit he'd started.

***

"Nigga, what you doing out here? Yo' shit plastered on every news station there is! I got this shit covered, brah. Get ghost. Twelve is hot around this muthafucka and I need you to shake."

Skip, Dex's right hand was shitting bricks as he stepped out of his whip. Dex wasn't worried about anything jumping off for shooting the lame-ass nigga Ailani was laying up with. He wasn't about that life because that shit hadn't made the news. As far as the drug shit, all they had was video of him going in the residence; nothing on the drugs that was found. Ailani was going to take all the heat for that shit.

He'd met up with his lawyer and was going to turn himself in once he made sure his money was right. They had nothing to hold him for and he was confident about that because his fingerprints weren't going to be found on any of the packages; only Ailani's.

"I'm going to handle that shit soon as I leave here. I needed to come check on my money flow before I do. There's no telling what the fuck they're going to try to hit me with." Dex leaned against his ride and crossed his legs.

"What about that nigga we got at the other day? You heard anything about his condition?"

"No, and I don't give a damn about that shit. He ain't about this life, so he better take that slug and keep living. That nigga don't want those types of problems. The only thing I'm concerned about is getting out of this drug jam. Anyway, how's business around here?"

"Everything is cool. We're selling this shit like hotcakes. You already know, I'm all about the moola, baby. Ain't shit slowing up long as the fiends are out and I'm in charge. Your business is in good hands, nigga."

"That's what I like to hear. Check it, I don't know what's in store for me. On some real shit, I want you to hold this shit down. Run it with an iron fist as if I was standing right beside you. Take today's keep to the crib. Melissa and the girls are there, but be respectable of my shit. In other words, knock this time muthafucka."

Skip laughed because the last time he went over to do a drop, Melissa had just gotten out of the shower and had a barely-there towel wrapped around her body. He used his key and got an eyeful. Unbeknownst to Dex, Skip had been lusting over his baby mama ever since. Hell, if his boy wasn't hitting that ass, somebody needed to help her in that department. That somebody was going to be him one day.

"I got you, bro. But if she don't answer, I can use the key, right?"

"She gon' answer. If she doesn't, then yeah. Then you call and let me know because I'm gon' need to know where the fuck she at with my shorties." At that point, Dex's phone started ringing and it was his lawyer. "Yo, I gotta roll. I'll be in touch and if I don't get back with you, that means that locked my ass down. You know what to do if that end up being the case."

"Fa sho'. You got this, Dex. Like you said, they don't got shit on you," Skip said dapping him up.

Dex hurried to the driver side of his whip and hit his lawyer back. "Cunningham, I'm on the road now."

"Okay, I'll be outside waiting when you pull up. I hope you're not nervous. I got you. Now, get here, I have shit to do."

Driving down the highway with his stomach clutched, Dex was glad his lawyer hung up because he wasn't ready to admit how nervous he really was. Even trying to play the hard role with Skip was easy. The last thing Dex wanted to do was show a weak side of his typical self. In his mind, he was going to go in and come back out a free man, but in the back of his mind, he knew the pigs could lock a nigga up because *they* believe he was guilty. Hopefully, that wouldn't be the case.

Derek Cunningham was waiting outside the precinct in a tailored suit just like he said he would be. When Dex stepped out of his car, Cunningham met him halfway with his hand held out. They shook hands and Cunningham released his grip and wiped his palm on his pants leg.

"Shake that shit off, man. If they smell fear on you, they're going to pounce. The evidence they have is circumstantial. It's Ailani's word against yours and she has been caught in one lie when she stated the drugs belonged to her ex. We got this; trust me."

Dex nodded his head and took a deep breath. The two entered the building and Cunningham did all the talking. Dex was escorted to an empty interrogation room as his lawyer followed close behind. They sat in the cool room about fifteen minutes before a detective enter with a file in hand.

"Nice of you to finally come in to talk to me Mr. Hinton. You're a tough man to track down. For a minute, I thought you ran on me. By the way, I'm Detective Lemon," he said with an outstretched hand.

Dex looked at it without moving an inch to shake it. With a low chortle, the detective unbuttoned his suit jacket and took a seat on the other side of the table.

"So that we're on the same page, you are aware that there's a warrant out for your arrest for the drugs found on at the residence of Ailani Denton and Malik Daniels, correct?"

"Yeah, that's what I was told. I'm here to let you know, I don't know nothing about any drugs. What those folks had going on didn't have anything to do with me."

"Are you saying you've never been inside of that residence, Mr. Hinton?" Detective Lemon asked.

"First of all, don't try to put words in my mouth. It's obvious I've been there. Otherwise, my face wouldn't be all over the damn news. Second of all, I was there for one purpose and one purpose only, and that was to fuck something," Dex laughed. "If I would've known I would be implemented in some drug shit, I wouldn't have been there."

Detective Lemon's face turned red as he cleared his throat. "According to Ailani, the drugs belong to you. We stand by her testimony because you are seen several times entering and leaving the residence with a duffle bag. Were there drugs in that bag, Mr. Hinton?"

"Again, I went to shorty's crib on several occasions. When you leave home for an overnight visit, Detective Lemon, don't you take a bag of clothes and other hygiene products with you? Don't even answer that. The bag was my thot bag, a'ight?"

"Thot bag?"

"Yeah, you know, women have hoe bags and men got thot bags. It's new lingo. I'll simplify it for you. That shit was an overnight bag. Plus, from my understanding, didn't Ailani say the drugs belonged to her man?" Detective Lemon was quiet for a minute. "See, you didn't think I knew about that shit, huh? See, she's lying somewhere, but y'all rolling with what she said to get at me. I've got a record from back in the day; I'll take that. What do y'all have on me in the last ten years? Not a damn thing, because I went legit a long time ago. That drug shit been a thing of my past."

"Mr. Hinton, you're right about your record. I've looked into it. I just don't believe the drug game is a thing of your past because here we are today," Detective Lemon said skimming his notepad. "When was the last time you've seen Miss Denton?"

"I believe about a month and a half ago."

"You didn't visit Miss Denton at the Central Regional. Detention Facility a few weeks ago?"

Cunningham's neck whipped around to look at his client because that was news to him. He'd told Dex to stay far away from Ailani. The shift in his eyes told Cunningham all he needed to know. His stupid ass did go to visit and the time to tell the truth was at that moment. That could really hurt him.

"I haven't been to see Ailani! Where did that come from? I didn't even know she was locked up," Dex snapped.

Detective Lemon smirk while sifting through his paperwork. Finding what he was looking for, he folded is hands on top of the table. Cunningham wanted to chop his client in the throat right there in front of the detective. He sat there lying, and Cunningham was certain the detective had proof of that. His client was digging himself in a hole and there would be nothing Cunningham to do to get him out of it.

"Mr. Hinton, I want you to think about the question I asked. I'm going to ask one more time and I want you to be truthful with me."

"I haven't been to anybody's prison, muthafucka!" Dex yelled.

Detective Lemon nodded his head and placed a piece of paper in front of Dex. "Is this not a copy of your Driver's license, Mr. Hinton? The date on this document shows that you were indeed at the prison to see Miss Denton." He then placed another sheet of paper on top of the last. "This document is proof that you signed the visitor sheet as well. If you want me to go a step forward, I know for a fact you threatened Ailani as well and made good on that very threat."

The color drained from Dex's face and he looked over at his attorney. Cunningham couldn't do anything except shake his head. Dex leg was bouncing a mile a minute under the table and his nervousness was in full display. Sweat was building up on his forehead and upper lip.

"See, Trisha Jackson is in solitary confinement and has gotten a few years added to her sentence for the beating she put on Ailani. There are witnesses that says as she was beating Ailani, your name kept coming up. Oh, the cell phone Trisha had, we have all the text logs and call logs indicating you put the hit out for Ailani. I'll be back." Detective Lemon stood as he collected his evidence and left the room.

Dex sat with his head down. He knew he had fucked up. Cunningham stood and paced the floor angrily. "What the hell were you thinking going to that prison? On top of that, you had someone beat that woman up! You fucked yourself, Dex. That detective is going to come back in here and put a pair of silver bracelets on your ass and there's nothing I can do about it! Your stupid ass left me in the dark and now you're screwed."

The door opened before Dex could respond and two officers walked in. "Dexter Hinton, you are under arrest for the assault of Ailani Denton. There's also a warrant for your arrest for the murder of Harold "Big Man" Shaffer. Stand to your feet, turn around, and put your hands behind your back. You're definitely going to spend quite some time behind bars. I hope you got enough of the fresh air before you came in, because from now on, you will only get it for an hour a day," Detective Lemon gloated while watching another officer cuff the man he'd been looking for.

Dex did what he was told without a fight. He knew he fucked up and hoped Cunningham would fight to get him out of the predicament he put himself in. As the handcuffs were fastened around his wrists, Dex closed his eyes and the first thing he saw was his babies. A lone tear slid down his face as they led him away.

Chapter 19

The weeks flew past with a breeze and Malik's recovery was going very well. He still couldn't go back to work at the hospital and he has been quite depressed about it. Toni had done her best to keep him out of his funk by getting him out of the house. The time the two has spent together strengthened their relationship a lot. Toni got the chance to see the Hollywood Walk of Fame, strolled along Beverly Hills, and did a little bit of shopping, as well as spent time with her girls. Most of all, she kept Malik happy.

Toni had been doing a lot of research on properties in California so she could open her own Paralegal Services business. She'd been working hard online as if she was back at the firm in Chicago. Her days were actually ending about six or seven, but it didn't cut into the duties she put in place as the woman of Malik's house. He was blessed with breakfast, lunch, and dinner every day. Toni spoiled that man and he loved every bit of it.

Malik walked behind Toni as she sat at the desk working and wrapped his hand around her shoulders. "How's work going?"

"I'm hanging in there. My workload has increased since I've been here. Jacob must think I'm a damn robot. At times I feel he can't do anything for himself when I'm away," Toni said, shaking her head. "It's good that I can do my job sitting down. If I was one of the paralegals that went out to crime sites, I would never get any time off."

"Well, you're doing a damn good job. You are a natural with this working and taking care of home shit. You haven't missed a beat since you stepped onto California soil. I want to thank you for being here with me, keeping me occupied during my depression period because I can't work like I'm used to doing, and for not giving up by leaving when I needed time to myself. All of those things on top of leaving your priorities in Chicago to come here for me, means a lot."

Toni swiveled in the chair until she was facing Malik. "You don't have to thank me. Everything I've done is because I wanted to do it."

"I know," he said, bending down to kiss her lips. "Allow me to tell my woman how much I appreciate her, would you?'

"Have at it, pimp," Toni smirked.

"Get back to work. I'm about to whip up a couple of turkey paninis with a side of plain Lays potato chips. Isn't nothing like the things you make, but I want to cook for you for a change. You've been around here putting in work. I'm just waiting for the day you're barefoot and pregnant living here full- time. Speaking of which, when are you going to bless me with your presence on a permanent basis, Toni?"

Toni knew the time they'd spent together would allow the feelings they had for one another grow fonder. She didn't want to rush into a move then have to travel back and forth to get back to her cousin if needed. Malik seemed to understand her feelings on the subject, but she wondered how he would take it.

"I have things I need to work out as far as work is concerned. Plus, you know my situation with Tangie. I don't think leaving her permanently would be good for her. We will spend a lot of time together, Malik. There's no rush. I'm not going anywhere."

"We've talked about your cousin. I won't go into it again because I never want you to feel as if I'm being insensitive about the whole thing. As for your job, isn't working from home an option if you're doing the leg work all the way from here?"

"Malik, we're not about to play the twenty questions game. My cousin and I are for life and my job is one I've been with for the past seven years. I'm not turning my back on either one for a relationship that can end any day. There are levels to this shit and it takes time. I'm a woman that likes to have her ducks in a row before taking a drastic leap of faith. Please don't start putting pressure on me about this move when my life in Chicago hasn't been concluded."

Toni didn't mean to snap at him. When she pointed out she wasn't ready, that should've been the end of it. As much as Malik claimed to understand, Toni could tell he didn't understand at all. They were still in the dating stage of their relationship and he was thinking about knocking her up with bare feet. Kids weren't in the near future for Toni because she had no plans of being anybody's baby mama.

"Look, I'm sorry for raising my voice at you."

Malik turned to walk away but Toni wasn't going to let that happen. Her relationship with LaZeric was always disagreeing and going to bed without talking it out. She had no intentions of allowing that to happen again. They were adults, dammit, and communication was going to be key.

"Don't do that. I'm trying to talk and you're walking away as if I scolded you. Would you rather I feed you a sob story or keep it real? Don't respond to that," Toni said, taking a deep breath. "Malik, I will never tell you what you want to hear. I'm really enjoying what we have going on. Do I think we're ready to move in together? Sure I do, but the timing isn't right. Long distance relationships are challenging, I know. As long as we work at it together, there's nothing that can get in the way of what's to come. In the meantime, we will continue to get to know each other on every level and I will make sure the visits stay consistent. That's all we can do at this point."

Toni's voice softened, hoping he saw things the way she did. The solemn look in his eyes let her know he wasn't feeling what she said. Malik looked everywhere except at her and she didn't like it at all. Never letting go of his arm, she rubbed her thumb across his skin.

"Talk to me, Malik," Toni all but pleaded.

"What can I say? You're not ready and I can't force that on you. I'm here to let you know, many long-distance relationships don't work out the way you see it. There's the feeling of loneliness from missing the one that you want to be with. Not to mention, it leads to thoughts of filling that void with someone that's closer. Many long-distance relationships will end sooner or later and I feel it's a temporary thing for one or both parties involved. Where you have faith in it, I see destruction."

"Malik, if the only thing you can point out is the cons, then yeah, it won't work. I'm going to hit you with a few pros of the situation. Being away from one another can help the trust factor build between us. Being apart builds the flame of missing each other when we've been away for a period of time. We can continue to Facetime and call whenever we feel the need. On top of that, we will prepare ourselves for the moment we are in each other's space every day. Neither one of us is prepared for that; at least I'm not. It's been years since I've shared a place with anyone. I also want to give you time since you just came out of a live-in relationship."

"Whatever, Toni. Like it said, I won't force you into something you don't want." With that, Malik walked off in the direction of the kitchen.

Toni sat at the desk, staring at the wall. They'd just had their first disagreement, and it didn't go well.

Before she could dwell on it further, her phone rang. Reaching for the device, she quickly answered after seeing Tangie's name on the display.

"Hey, cousin! How are you?" Toni was happy to hear from her cousin and knew she would bring her back to a happy place; so she thought.

"Toni, where are you?" Tangie croaked out.

"I'm in California. What's wrong?" she asked as her hand started to shake. Tangie didn't sound well and she had no clue where the conversation was going to lead.

"I need you, Toni. What I'm doing is wrong and I want to get away from these drugs. You told me to come to you when I was ready."

"Yes, I've been waiting to hear those words come from you. I'll come back tomorrow. You need me," Toni said, tapping away on the keyboard to book her flight.

"Don't cut your trip short for me. I'll be alright until you come back."

"Nonsense. I'm coming back tomorrow. Go to Auntie's house and I'll be on my way soon as I get off the plane. Where are you?" Toni asked.

"I'm on 68th and Indiana at my homie's house. I'll stay here until you call to say you're back."

Hearing Tangie's location made the hairs rise on the back of Toni's neck. The conversation she'd had with LaZeric came back full force.

"No, I want you to get away from there. Go to the house and wait for me cousin, please," Toni begged.

"I don't feel like being ridiculed, Toni. I won't lie, I'm high as fuck and don't have time for the backlash. I'll go once my high comes down. I'm straight over here. I'll let you get back to what you were doing. I've held you on this phone long enough. I love you, cousin."

"I love you too, and I'll be there soon as I can. Be careful out there," Toni said.

Tangie ended the call and Toni immediately went to her call log to place a call she didn't really want to make. Hovering over LaZeric's name, she said "fuck it" in her head and pressed the button. As she listened to the phone ring, she was about to hang up when he answered.

"What a pleasure it is to see your name on my phone. How can I help you, Sexy?"

"This is not the type of call you may think it is, LaZeric. I need you to go to the spot you told me about and get Tangie away from there. She's high and is crying out for help. I don't want anything to happen to her. Tangie refuses to go to my aunt's, but I don't want her over there. If you can just take her to your house until tomorrow, I will come get her."

"Toni, Tangie isn't going to leave with me. That doesn't mean I won't try though. I just want you to know, it's a hit or miss. You're the only person she seems to listen to." LaZeric paused. "When I get off, I'll go over there and see what I can do."

"Thank you. I really appreciate you," Toni said sincerely.

"Would it be too much to ask if we can go out to dinner in the near future?"

"That won't be a good idea. Can we just stick to Tangie's situation please?"

LaZeric agreed to drop the subject and promised to go on 68th later. Ending the call, Toni didn't notice Malik standing in the doorway until he placed her lunch on the desk. She looked up and opened her mouth to say thanks, but Malik was glaring at the computer screen. The computer screen displayed her flight details for him to see.

"You're leaving tomorrow?" he asked.

"Yes, I got a phone call from Tangie and she needs me. She has finally reached out for help and I can't ignore her at a time like this. I've waited awhile to hear the words I heard a few minutes ago. I have to go to her soon as possible. I booked the flight while on the phone with her and I was coming to tell you afterwards."

"No, you called LaZeric; whoever that may be, to hold shit down before coming to me," Malik snapped.

"I had to reach out to someone that could reach my cousin since I'm not there. LaZeric knows the area she's in, so I reached out to him."

"Who is this person? I don't recall meeting him during my visit and I damn sure have never heard the name."

"He's my ex. Before you jump to conclusions, what he and I had has been over. You have nothing to worry about when it comes to LaZeric Jackson. One thing you will learn about me is that Toni never goes backwards. Once it's over, it's over."

Malik nodded his head, but didn't go further with his questioning. In the back of his mind, he had a feeling that LaZeric was part of the reason Toni wasn't ready to move to the West Coast. He wouldn't allow his assumptions to ruin the remaining time Toni was in town, but the truth would reveal itself in due time.

***

Toni and Malik spent the rest of the evening together, but the tension was thick. No matter what she said to him, he responded drily. She prepared a dinner of collard greens, sweet potatoes, cornbread, and fried chicken. The two of them sat at the table and ate silently. The awkwardness was something they hadn't experienced and Toni wasn't feeling it at all. After washing the dishes and watching Malik head to his mancave, Toni decided to call Baylei and Jordyn to tell them she was leaving the following morning.

The conversation was short-lived because the two of them were doing the complete opposite of what Toni was enduring; being lovey dovey with their men. Toni opened the door leading to the lower part of the house and was greeted with the soulful sound of Shaun Milli's "Love Me".

See, I ain't got that much time left
'Cause I give you my all and all you give me is your ass to kiss
What I'ma do with it?
I think it's best if I move to the left
'Cause I know that somebody waiting on all this love I gotta give
I'm wondering...
When you gon' me?
'Cause I'm tired of waiting patiently, baby
When you gon' love me?
And if you ain't gon' love me like I L-O-V-E
You should tell me

Hearing Malik sing the lyrics to the song with his chest caused Toni to go right back up the stairs and the tears ran from her eyes like waterworks. Malik had the wrong impression of her feelings for him. There's was no doubt in her mind that she loved him as well, which had nothing to do with her picking up and leaving my family behind. Toni went into the bedroom, grabbed her night clothes and heading to the shower.

She stood in the mirror to brush her teeth and the minute she looked at her reflection, she started crying again. Toni wasted no time stripping out of her clothes and stepping into the tub. Turning the water on the hottest setting she could stand, she stood under the water and let the tears fall freely. Her soul was cleansed of everything that was weighing on her shoulders. From Tangie, to LaZeric popping back up, and the new dilemma between her and Malik. It was all too much for her to deal with all at once.

To allow the pressures of life to weigh down on one at once could cause a person to break down to mere pieces. There were times where you couldn't solve all the problems around you in a short period. Many things required time to work itself out. Others could be taken care of in due time. Toni had burdens that she had no control over taking a toll on her inner being. With Tangie reaching out for help, that was going to be her first priority. There was no telling when she would get the chance again.

Washing her body several times, Toni dried off, pulled the oversized T-shirt over her body, and exited the bathroom with the clothes she'd taken off in hand. She went around the room gathering her belongings and packed her bag. After all the crying she did to cleanse her mind, Toni crawled in the bed and set her alarm so she wouldn't oversleep for her flight back home.

"Toni, your alarm is going off. Get up so you can get dressed and to the airport," Malik whispered in her ear as he shook her awake.

Shifting positions, Toni opened her eyes and stared deeply into his. She could tell he hadn't gotten any sleep the previous night because his eyes were bloodshot red. The alcohol was seeping through his pores and there was no way he'd be able to accompany her to the airport. The concern was evident on her face and Malik saw it the moment it appeared.

"Don't worry, I've arranged for Chade and Baylei to take you to the airport," he said, rising up from the side of the bed.

"Malik, I'm sorry if I gave you the impression that I didn't love you." He paused his steps, but didn't turn around to face her. "Knowing I was wasn't ready to move here, I held my feelings at bay. Doing that, when our relationship was fragile enough to let concerns like the ones you're having ease in wasn't the best choice. Neither one of us has verbally voiced our feelings, and that was fine with me because going with the flow makes the heart grow fonder. I want you to know from me, that I love you more than you give me credit for, Malik."

"I love you too, Toni. Hear me and hear me good. Tell that nigga to keep his muthafuckin' hands to himself. You're mine, and I'm not giving you up that easy. Our time will come and I'm going to be here waiting with open arms. Go home and take care of your business, baby. Just don't forget that I'm a plane ride away and I won't be calling to give any heads up. The trust you spoke of is in full effect. Now, get yo' ass up and get yourself together."

Toni smiled as she watched him walk from the room. She wanted to go suck his dick after that shit, but time was of the essence.

The doorbell rang as soon as she started descending the steps a half hour later. Malik answered the door and Chade walked in, giving him a brotherly hug. They both looked back at Toni as she stepped off the last stair. Chade took her bag and left back out the door, giving them time to say their goodbyes.

"I'll call you soon as I land and again when I get to my aunt's house," Toni said wiping at his chapped lips. "I'm going to miss you, Malik Daniels."

"You act like we're never going to see one another again. I'm always going to be right here," he said, tapping two fingers on the left side of her chest. "I'm going to miss you too, Miss Daniels." Malik brought his head down, kissing her lips tenderly, keeping his tongue to himself. The alcohol he consumed the night before had his mouth dry as cotton. "I'll be waiting on your call. Take care of your business and tell me how it went."

"Will do," Toni said, hugging him tightly.

She left the house, constantly looking back at the man that she loved. Malik watched the car until they were long gone.

The entire ride to the airport, Toni was quiet. Her nerves were all over the place because she didn't know what she would be facing once she made it to her aunt's house.

The ride to the airport ended fairly quickly and she was standing outside of Chade's car crying with her friend. It had been a while since the three of them weren't home together. Baylei and Jordyn offered to accompany her back to Chicago, but she declined.

"Call me if you need me, sis," Baylei said, wiping the tears from Toni's eyes. "Everything will be alright. Here's my keys. Take my car from the airport. I'll send money for the payment."

"I got you and I love you, Lei. Don't worry about sending money. I got it. Thank you. I'll talk to you later. Thank you for the ride, Chade," she said, leaning through the window.

"No problem. Hang in there and let us know if there's anything you need. We will be there next week to move Baylei anyway. But if we have to come before hand, we will."

Chade let her know her support system was solid and that meant so much to Toni. Nodding her head at him, she turned back to her friend and hugged her tightly before making her way into the airport.

It took a while to get through security and her flight was ready to board by the time she got to the gate. Once Toni was seated, she placed her earbuds in her ears and went to sleep through the entire flight.

After getting Baylei's car, Toni did a cool hundred to her aunt's house. She tried calling Tangie to no avail and the knots returned to her stomach. As she sat at a red light, she decided to check the texts that she had received while on the flight. There was one from LaZeric from the night before and her stomach dropped.

LaZeric said by the time he got to the house on 68th, Tangie was nowhere to be found. Toni hoped like hell she was waiting at her aunt's house when she arrived.

It took about forty-minutes to make it through traffic and Toni was on the brink of breaking down. The music she played didn't do anything to calm her down. But she was able to maneuver through traffic without causing an accident.

Pulling into her aunt's driveway, she barely got the key out the ignition before she was hopping out of the car. Instead of knocking, Toni used her key to enter. Her aunt was in the kitchen doing what she did best; cooking breakfast. Something she did every morning.

"Toni, what are you doing here? I thought you were still in California."

"I was, but Tangie called me yesterday saying she was tired of living her life doing drugs and needed my help. Have you heard from her?"

"No. I haven't seen or heard from my child in a couple of days. Is she alright, Toni?" her aunt asked with worry in her eyes.

"I don't know. I'm about to go out to see if I can find her. When I talked to her, she sounded like she was ready to get right. I have to get to her. I'll call and let you know if I found her or not."

"Be careful out there, baby."

Aunt Brenda walked over to her niece and gathered her arms around her. Since Toni was younger, she could always tell when she was at her breaking point. That day was no different. The instant her arms touched her niece, she fell to pieces.

"She said she would be here waiting for me," Toni wailed. "I know she wants the help, but she can't stop chasing that high! I wish I knew what to do to get through to her. Tangie is my everything. I won't lose her to this shit, Auntie! She's bigger than the drugs that's thinking for her. I wish I could've prevented this from happening! I saw all the signs and did nothing! Taking her word that she was alright instead of doing something."

Toni sobs caught the attention of her uncle and he joined in on the hug that her aunt initiated. "Toni, you can't blame yourself for the road Tangie decided to take. We all saw the changes, but there was nothing we could've done. Everyone grieves in their own way. Tangie decided to experiment with pills to take her away from the hurt she was experiencing. All we can do from this point is pray."

Toni pulled back in rage. "No, that's all y'all can do! I'm going to help my cousin to the best of my ability. If y'all didn't ridicule her about her addiction and took more time to help, we wouldn't be where we are today! I'm not giving shit to God! I'm going to do whatever it takes for my muthafuckin' cousin!"

Toni left, slamming the door behind her. She knew the words that spewed from her mouth were out of anger but that was how she was feeling. Hopping in Baylei's car, she backed out of the driveway with a slight headache strumming at her temples. The radio came on and Bruno Mars's "Grenade" filled the car.

I'd catch a grenade for ya
Throw my hands on a blade for ya
I'd jump in front of train for ya
You know I'd do anything for ya
Oh, oh I would go through all this pain
Take a bullet straight through my brain
Yes, I would die for ya, baby
But you won't do the same.

That's exactly how she felt about her cousin and it was the reason she was going so hard for her. Toni hoped like hell there was still hope and it wasn't too late. She went to the block LaZeric had said he'd spotted Tangie, but the block was deserted. Other than that location, Toni didn't know where else to look. Instead, she kept driving around that neighborhood, but she didn't see her cousin anywhere. Toni owed her aunt and uncle and apology, but they wouldn't get it that day. She jumped on the expressway an hour later and went home. She was exhausted from the flight, crying, and driving around.

When she reached her house, she parked the car next to her own and got out after grabbing her bag. As she climbed the stairs, she spotted a figure in the corner of the porch. Fear filled her body and she turned to run back to the car.

"Toni, don't leave me here."

The sound of Tangie's voice pleading stopped her instantly. She ran back to the porch and by that time, Tangie was standing at her full height. She could barely stand, so she sat on the top stoop of the porch. Toni saw for herself that her cousin was high as fuck. She was higher than she'd ever seen her before. Tangie could barely hold her head up. It kept falling to her chest and it brought the tears back to Toni's eyes.

"Tangie, how did you get out here?" Toni asked.

"My homie brought me. I needed to get away from that house. Cousin—"

Her words faded out and she nodded until her phone fell from her hand. Tangie scrambled to pick it up and laughed. She started talking off the wall and the shit didn't make any sense at all. The sight before her made Toni mad as hell.

"What the fuck are you on, Cuz? That's not a pop pills nod. Pills don't do shit like that. It has to be more than just pills."

"Nah, that's all it is," Tangie slurred. "I'm just tired from being up all night."

"Tell that shit to somebody that's going to believe it because I don't. That's a dope nod!" Toni was crying so hard her vision blurred. When Tangie nodded out again in the middle of her rant, she lost it. Toni reached back and slapped the shit out of Tangie. The hit didn't faze her and she actually laughed, looking at her cousin through low lids.

"Get yo' ass in here and lay down! You don't need to be out and about like this, Cuz."

Toni fumbled with her keys as they fell from her hand. Finally getting the door opened, she stepped to the side so Tangie could walk through before her. Instead of going to the spare bedroom up-stairs, Tangie went straight for the couch.

"Aht, aht! When I said go lay down, that meant upstairs and to a bed!"

"I'm good, Toni. I promise," Tangie slurred, but made her way to the stairs.

Toni followed close behind until her cousin was in the bedroom sitting on the bed. She watched her cousin for a little while before going in her room to get out of the clothes she had on. As she dis-robed, she could hear Tangie walking back and forth in the room. Toni knew she was antsy and was going to give her a bit of time by herself. Once she was undressed, she retrieved her phone from her purse to call her aunt.

"Did you find her, Toni?" she asked anxiously.

"No, she found me. Tangie was sitting on my porch when I got home. She's alright. I set her up in the guest bedroom and I will bring her over there in the morning. I'm too tired to drive back to the city."

"That's fine. As long as she's with you, I can sleep tonight. Please don't let her leave that house, Toni. Is she high? And don't lie to me."

"Yes, she is. Auntie, Tangie is doing more than pills. I can't say what she's doing, but it's more than what she's saying. We will figure this out. In the meantime, I'll be looking for a facility because she needs to go soon as possible. She's too far gone to go willingly. I got this. Get some sleep and I'll tell you what I've found out."

"Okay, baby. Thank you for calling me."

"Auntie, I owe you an apology—" Toni started to say.

"No, you don't. You said what was on your mind and I'm not mad about it. You have my baby there with you. Talk to her, Toni. She will listen to you. I love you."

Toni told her aunt she loved her too and took her laptop from her bag to start looking for a rehab center. Finding Tangie help was her top priority. Every facility she called stated they would be able to admit her cousin, but they couldn't force her to stay. In other words, if Toni checked her in, Tangie would be able to check herself right the fuck out. She was told the same thing Malik had already told her when she said she was going to find a facility to put Tangie in. That left Toni no choice but to try and talk her cousin into going in for the help she said she was ready for the night before.

As she walked down the hall, Toni could hear Tangie talking lowly behind the door she had closed. She knocked lightly on the door, and it took her cousin a few minutes to invite her in. Toni entered and sat on the end of the bed as she watched her cousin pace back and forth.

"Come sit down, Tangie," she said lowly. "Tangie, come sit down!" Toni yelled.

Tangie looked over her shoulder at her cousin, but she kept moving about the room. Toni was getting dizzy watching her move around in circles. As she pulled her legs onto the bed, Toni played back the conversation they had when Tangie called while she was in California. Toni was going to remind her cousin why she was home ahead of time.

"Tangie, let's talk about the help you wanted yesterday. I came home to help you figure it out."

"I don't need help, Cuz. I'm good. All I need is some sleep and I'll be cool. When I called you, I wasn't in my right state of mind," she said, sniffing loudly. "I got some candy, Cuz, you want some?" Tangie asked pulling out a bag of Hi-Chews.

She loved those taffy-ass candies and they were good as shit. Had damn near everybody eating those things, and she didn't turn down the offer to snack on them that day either. Toni slowly chewed the taffy and laughed because Tangie ate three to her one. Her cousin automatically started laughing too, but Toni wanted to get back to the subject at hand.

"So, you said when you called me you weren't in your right state of mind, right? What do you call the state you are in right now, Tangie?"

"I'm just chillin', to be honest. I'm mellow as hell, cuz. Nothing to worry about."

"We've talk about this before and I want to get you the help you need. You said it yourself that you're tired of using. Let's start the process so you can get rid of the demon that you're fighting every day. Please don't say you're good because you're not, Cuz. I've seen you go from vibrant to a person trapped in a shell. There are days when you are yourself, but lately, I haven't seen that person. I want my cousin back!"

Tangie was quiet for a moment and Toni knew she made her think about what she said.

"You're right. I haven't been the Tangie that y'all know and love. I didn't choose this life, Toni. This life chose me! I may not be the person that I once was, but what is there for me to do? The drugs follow me every day of my fuckin' life and there's no getting away from them. I can't beat this shit, okay? I've tried and I'll tell you, when I'm high, I don't think about none of the shit that haunts me on a daily. But when I'm sober, life hits me like a ton of bricks! You don't think what I have to live through every hour of the day affects me! Well, it does!"

Tangie finally sat down and the tears filled the rims of her eyes, but they didn't fall. She got up and grabbed the candy she placed on the dresser and started eating them one by one. Out of the blue, she started laughing. Tangie laughed so hard that she doubled over clutching her stomach.

"Do you remember when we snuck out the house and went to the party out west and came back drunk as hell? Your mama was ready to beat the shit out of both of us. She was so mad she couldn't even fuck us up."

"Yeah, we dodged a bullet with that one. We spent the night laughing and giggling until she came and told us to go to sleep before she beat the shit out of us. I never fell asleep so fast in my life," Toni laughed.

Tangie laughed along with her, but then the laughter turned to loud sobs. Toni got up to console her cousin, but Tangie shook her head no vigorously. Allowing her the space she needed, Toni sat back down and waited. It took ten minutes before her cousin caught her breath to talk.

"I miss them so much, Toni. If they hadn't been killed, I wouldn't be in the fucked-up position I'm in. Am I wrong for grieving for them, even though both of my parents are alive and well?" Toni opened her mouth to respond, but Tangie wasn't finished. "That damn girl got away scot-free while we had to bury my aunt and uncle. Seeing them lying in those damn coffins was something I never want to see again. I see that shit every day in my sleep! And what do I do? Go out and find some drugs to make that shit disappear! This can't be fuckin' life, man!"

"I know, Tangie. That entire day plays in my mind all the time, so I know how you feel. I have to go through that shit 'til this day and it's been four years and counting."

"Stop saying you know how it feels, because you don't! At least not the way I have experienced it. This shit will forever be a nightmare to me. I don't know how to get the images out of my head without taking something to cope with the pain that I feel constantly. Toni, I'm so sorry. You have always been there whenever

I've called you. Never turned your back on me and was always willing to talk no matter what time I called. I love you for that, Toni. I owe you for life, cousin."

Toni got to her feet and ran to her cousin. She hugged her tightly until the hug was returned. They stood that way for God knows how long. When Toni went to step back, Tangie pulled her even closer, grabbing the back of her shirt. Tangie's tears soaked the shoulder of Toni's shirt, but that was the least of her worries. Her cousin let out some of the pain she had bottled up inside and she believed that was a start.

"Tangie, you don't owe me anything."

"I do," she wailed.

Toni stepped out of Tangie's grasp, but held on to her arms. "Okay, you can pay me back by calling me to let me know you are alright. Is that a deal?" Toni asked as she looked into her cousin's eyes.

"I can do that. Now go lay down, because you look tired as shit. I'm going to get some sleep myself. Then I'll get up and make us some hot wings and fries. Extra spicy." Tangie smiled.

"I'm holding you to that shit too. I better smell that sauce in the air when I wake up."

"I got you."

Toni went to her room after pulling the door up to the room her cousin was in. She called her aunt, Malik, and Baylei before crawling under the sheets to sleep.

Waking up to nothing but silence, Toni listened for the sound of Tangie pacing, but it never came. She got up from her bed and raced to the guest room. When she got to the doorway, her heart dropped. Sitting in the middle of the bed was a note written in Tangie's handwriting.

Cousin,

Thank you for always looking out for me. You slapped the fuck outta me, but I don't hold that against you. That's love if I've never seen it before. You had every reason to react the way you did. I still love you though. I know you're fuming right now because I left as soon as I heard you breathing evenly. Don't call my mama and tell her I left. I promise to go by their house in the morning. The bond we have is forever and I love you always.

Tangie.

P.S I'll call you so you can hear my voice. Smooches

Toni fell to the floor and cried until she couldn't cry anymore. Tangie was out there bad and there was nothing she could do to save her. The only thing she could do was wait for her to check in.

Chapter 20

Driving through the streets for over a week, Christine did a great job evading the police. She knew the time was going to come for her to get caught. Surprisingly, the young woman she hijacked hadn't reported her car stolen. After taking her ID and taking her home, Christine threatened to gut her like a fish if she opened her mouth. She'd scoped out Cedars Sinai every day and she hadn't seen Malik's car. There was no way to figure out where he lived because she refused to allow Ailani out to help. Doing that was just like giving herself up voluntarily to the police, and that would never happen.

Christine made one last attempt at going to the hospital. When she spotted the vehicle she was looking for, she did a happy dance. Parking a few cars back from Malik's designated spot, she threw the car in park and cut the engine. It was going to be a long wait because she didn't know what time he would come out.

"Let me out!" Ailani's voice echoed in Christine's head.

"Shut up, whiny-ass bitch. You the reason we're in this predicament. All you had to do was steal his money and leave the damn state. Instead, you got greedy and started messing around with a drug dealer thinking you would be able to do the same to him and keep the doctor. Silly you, because that shit backfired on your goofy ass. Dex used you to hold his drugs and paid you crumbs." Christine laughed. "But you lied and blamed the wrong one because you were mad. It's okay, Boo-Boo Kitty, I'm gonna handle this one for you. Dex is in jail, so he will get his day sooner or later. Until then, sit back, lil baby, and watch me work."

Christine took a nice gulp of tequila and smiled when Ailani's voice faded away. Ailani took the pills to keep Christine away, but she didn't like alcohol because that brought out the Bad Bitch every time. She sipped and waited for over an hour before she spotted Malik coming out of the hospital in his white lab coat.

"Damn, he still looks good enough to eat. No wonder lil stupid didn't want to let him go. And look how that log's bouncing off his thigh! Maybe I need to fuck on something before I slit his throat." Christine laughed wickedly as she started the car.

Malik backed out and she followed him slowly. Christine was drinking the liquor like it was water while trying to figure out how she was going to get revenge on Malik. The alcohol had her swerving out of the lane and seeing everything double. She was officially drunk, but had to complete the mission.

Christine followed Malik on to the highway and turned the air conditioner on full blast to try and sober up. The alcohol was making its way through her bloodstream, making it hard to see things as they were. The lines on the road were moving faster than she was driving and it made her nervous, but she kept up with Malik's car. She was lucky because there weren't too many cars out at that time of the night.

Beeeeeeeep! A car horn had her pulling her car hard to the right because she had veered into the left lane. The driver gave her the middle finger and sped past her. Christine laughed and returned the gesture. "Stupid ass! Learn how to drive!" she screamed.

Christine raised the bottle to her lips and took her eyes off the road for a split second. That was a second too long because the car eased into the right lane, barely missing the car she'd cut off. The blaring of a horn jolted her eyes back to the road, but it was too late. The car slammed into the side median with a loud bang. Her head hit the steering wheel hard. She screamed out in pain, spilling the alcohol as the bottle fell from her hands. The air bag deployed and hit her square in the chest.

Trying to reach for the door handle to get out, she couldn't move an inch. Tears streamed down her face from the excruciating pain that traveled up her legs. Looking down, she saw the metal from the front end of the car piercing her legs through the blood that rolled in her eyes. Christine knew at that point she had fucked up. There was nowhere to run and the pain she was in let her know she was not running away from the scene.

Several people got out of their cars to help and she saw a woman on her phone. The police would be there soon and she needed somebody to get her out of the car. Malik ran from his car that he'd pulled onto the shoulder to help. Christine smiled as he got closer. When he looked inside to figure out how to get her out, she grabbed him by the shirt with her left hand.

"Malik, help me," she slurred out.

The scent of alcohol hit him in the face, but it was the voice that caused him to pause for a minute. "Ailani?" he asked shocked. "What the hell did you do?"

"I'm not Ailani! Help me out of here so I can leave!" she sneered.

"Your legs are pinned. You're not getting out of here on your own or with my help. Don't try to move, or you will cause more damage than there already is. You will get out of here, Ailani; I promise." Malik checked her vitals and they were strong, but she was bleeding profusely and it was probably from the alcohol in her system.

"Stop calling me Ailani! My name is Christine!"

Malik was bewildered because he knew the woman sitting in the rubble was indeed the woman he'd spent the past four years with. The words her mother spoke came back full force. Ailani proved at that point that she was for sure crazier than a muthafucka. Sirens could be heard in the far distance and the highway was jammed packed with angry motorist that were trying to get home or wherever they were headed.

"Just get me out of here and I promise I won't kill you like I planned, Malik. I can't go back to jail. That's the reason I convinced Ailani to leave. That's not where we belong. Help me get my legs out. They're going numb," Christine cried.

"There's, there's nothing I can do to get you out. Stay calm; the ambulance is almost here. They will help you."

"Nooooooo, you have to help me dammit! You owe me, Malik! If it wasn't for you, I wouldn't have been in jail in the first place," Christine screamed like a madwoman.

"Aye, man. She bat shit crazy. You know her?" a guy that had avoided the single car collision asked.

"Unfortunately, yes. And you're right, she is crazy."

"Fuck all y'all! If I make it out of this, Malik—"

"They gon' lock your ass up where you belong," Malik snapped back as he backed away from the car. "Save your energy. You're going to need it."

A fire trucks, an ambulance, and the police finally made their way to the front of the accident site. Christine was yelling at the top of her lungs and the blood was flowing from her forehead a mile a minute. Malik didn't know why he didn't try to stop the blood flow, but then again, he did. Deep down he hoped she'd pass out.

"Get back! Let us through," a firefighter yelled as he pushed his way through the crowd. He examined the interior of the car and turned around. "We need the jaws of life. There's no other way to get her out!"

"I'm going to kill you, Malik! I put that on Ailani's life!" Christine laughed with blood on her teeth.

"You are Ailani, crazy ass!" he muttered, walking away.

"Hey, I need you to stay on the scene. You're a witness," one of the officers said before Malik could get too far.

"No problem. I'll be in my car," he said, shaking his head.

Malik sat in his car and decided there was no way he would leave the site. Ailani needed to be put away for good, and he was the one that had all the information to make that happen.

Chapter 21

Selena had been at her mom's since she walked out on Samir. He knew he was wrong for denying his infidelity, but that was the only way he would be able to keep his wife by his side - or so he thought. When he went to Miami, it was for business. He took Lavita along because Selena wasn't feeling well. Taking another woman on a business trip wasn't the best idea, but what his wife didn't know couldn't hurt.

Samir had been dealing with Lavita for a few months and her love box drew him in. She became his side chick instantly. He never planned to make her anything more than that, but obviously, Lavita didn't see it that way. When Selena showed him the picture of him in Miami, he almost pissed on himself. She held on to that secret for months, never letting him know she even knew about it.

Samir had been walking around like a sick puppy. The house he shared with his wife and their six-month-old daughter, Sevyn, was too quiet for his liking. Every time he called his wife, she would send him to voicemail until he asked about Sevyn. That was the only time Selena would call him on video, so he could talk to his daughter and tell her how much he missed her. Sevyn's toothless smile always took Samir to a happy place and it was part of the reason he used her as the code word to get Selena on the line.

Samir was a manager at Wells Fargo Bank and Lavita was one of his lead tellers. Their relationship was under the radar in the workplace, but when Selena showed him the picture, which he knew Lavita had sent, he automatically found a way to get rid of her ass. Doing some digging, he found out Lavita was stealing from the clients' accounts and transferring funds into her own personal account. Samir had to wait until she did it again because the incidents he found were old.

He went about his day as if nothing was wrong, but he didn't flirt and do all that husband/wife shit at work anymore. Lavita had hit him up a few times and Samir ignored her. She wasn't worth losing his wife over. Since Selena knew about his infidelities, he wanted to do whatever it took to get his family back. Samir's phone chimed, indicating he had a text. He sat thinking without moving to grab his phone, until the chimes started coming through back-to-back.

Malik: It's Saturday and I need to talk. Come to my crib.

Chade: What's going on, bro?

Sanji: Oh yeah, I've been waiting on this shit! I'm there, what time?

Vincent: Man, keep me posted, I just got back to Chicago

Chade: Nigga you may as well move back to that muthafucka! Chaya got yo' ass pussy whipped LOL

Vincent: Fuck you! Chaya been on some sneaky shit and I have to keep an eye on her

Chade: You sound stupid as hell. Don't you have a job, nigga? If you lose that muthafucka I'm not paying none of your bills while you in the Windy City being a stalker. Whatever y'all got going on, don't put your hands on my sister!

Malik: Text that nigga about that shit on his time! I need y'all to get to my crib!

Ahmad: I'll be there. Like Sanji said, what time?

Malik: Now!

Samir laughed, got up from the couch and went upstairs to take care of his hygiene. Malik sounded as if his life was depending on the meet-up. They hadn't gotten together since the blow up at his house the last time, but Samir needed to get out of the house. As he stepped into the bathroom, his phone rang. It was Lavita. He let it go to voicemail because he didn't have anything to say to her unless it was work-related.

While brushing his teeth, Samir thought about any way he could to get Selena to forgive him. It was like trying to find a needle in a haystack and nothing came to mind. Maybe the guys could help out once Malik revealed what was going on with him. After showering and trimming his goatee, Samir went to his closet and grabbed a white tee and a pair of black joggers. He slipped on some boxers and put on his clothes before slipping his feet in a pair of black and white Jordans. Samir decided to send Selena a text asking to come over to see Sevyn.

My Wife: Hey, can I come over to see Sevyn today?

Samir hated the state of their marriage. He was used to going into the nursery to love on his daughter. Selena was always walking around with her ass hanging from under a T-shirt or a small pair of shorts. That was always a sight to see and almost every time ended up being a great sex session for the both of them. Three years of marriage, a beautiful baby girl, and he had to get caught cheating with a woman he didn't have any feelings for. Samir knew he fucked up and needed to make the shit right.

Snatching his keys from the dresser along with his phone and wallet, Samir made his way down the stairs and out of the house. He hopped in his truck and put on his seatbelt before putting it in drive. With his foot on the brake, Samir pulled his vibrating phone from his pocket. It was Selena calling on Facetime. He smiled big as he answered the video call, but was disappointed when he found himself looking at the ceiling.

"I figured I'd give you a call instead of texting. Today isn't a good day for you to come over to see Sevyn. I have plans to take her out and I don't know when we will be back. How about we meet up at the park tomorrow and you can spend time with her then?"

Samir was pissed, but he didn't let it show. Selena had every excuse in the book as to why he couldn't physically see his daughter. She was really making him suffer, but the shit he did had nothing to do with the relationship he had with his child. He would let her think she had one up on him for the time being though.

"That's fine. Are y'all okay?" Samir asked.

"Yeah, Sevyn is fine. You don't have to inquire about me," Selena sassed.

"Okay. Well, I'll talk to you later when I call to tell Sevyn goodnight."

Samir was going to play the game with her. He took his foot off the brake and drove toward Malik's crib. The warm wind blew through the window as he continued to hold his phone, even though

Selena didn't respond to his last statement. He could hear Sevyn's coos and was enjoying every bit of it.

"Where are you going?" Selena asked curiously.

Bad as Samir wanted to be petty, he kept it one hundred with her. Honesty was the best policy, right? "I'm on my way to meet up with guys," Samir said, getting straight to the point.

"Yeah, okay. The guys." Doubt was evident in the words she spewed as her lips were probably twisted to the side.

"If you don't believe me, you can always track my location. It still works, Love."

"Whatever, Samir. I have to finish getting ready so, bye."

She didn't wait for him to say another word before ending the video call. Samir laughed it off because he had brought everything that was happening on himself.

It didn't take long for him to get to Malik's crib. Pulling into the driveway, he noticed Sanji and Chade's car already there. Samir got out of his truck and jogged up the steps. He rang the doorbell repeatedly, knowing it was going to piss his boy off.

"I should've known it was your dumb ass," Malik said, swinging the door open. "Get in here!"

They gave each other dap and Samir stepped into the house. "What the hell was so important that you called us over here?"

"Man, once everybody gets here, I'll tell y'all all about it," Malik said solemnly. "All I'm gon' say is, the shit was wild. There's some wings, pizza, beer, and other drinks in the kitchen. Sanji and Chade are out back shooting hoops while we wait on Ahmad."

The doorbell rang just as Malik finished talking. He went to the door and pulled it open to let Ahmad in. Samir studied his boy and saw nothing but sadness. Even though Ahmad was smiling, it didn't reach his eyes.

"Long time no see. How's things going with you?" Samir said, meeting his friend with a brotherly hug.

"Man, shits been rough, but I'm hanging in there. I've been burying myself in work. This ain't about me though. Let's see what's going on with this nigga first. It's his time to shine." Ahmad laughed.

It was good to see Ahmad, but Samir could tell shit was weighing down heavy on him. The way his relationship ended with Chasity was fucked up, but it was good that Ahmad found out before he committed to her trifling ass.

The three of them walked out into Malik's huge backyard and right away, they could tell there was money on the line with the one-on-one basketball game that was in play.

"Take that shit! Three pointers all day on yo' ass!" Chade boasted as Sanji checked the ball to him. "You can't even lift those strong-ass arms while you out here betting against the kid." Chade dribbled the ball through his legs before stepping back to shoot it towards the hoop. The ball sank, hitting nothing but net. "Pay me my muthafuckin' money! I told you before you made the bet, you wasn't ready for this, Mr. Fireman." Chade laughed with his hand held out.

"It's cool," Sanji said, reaching into his pocket and pulling out two hundred-dollar bills and handing them to his cocky friend. "That shit ain't nothing to a nigga like me."

The two men walked over to the table where their friends were laughing about the ending of their game and dapped up. Chade took one of the towels Malik had laid out for him and Sanji, wiping the sweat from his face. Sitting back drinking and making small talk until the hoopers could catch their breaths, Samir couldn't help smiling as he watched who he considered his brothers all together.

Back in college, they were tight as thieves and over ten years later, they were just as tight. They had their ups and downs, but that shit got squashed faster than it got started. The brotherhood they formed was for life; any of them would agree. Malik clearing his throat brought Samir back to the yard.

"So, I wanted y'all to hear about the bullshit I went through Thursday night," Malik said, folding his hands on top of the table. "I got off work and was on the way to crib about ten o'clockish. A car slammed into the damn median and the driver fucked up her car. Why the hell I get to the car and it's Ailani?"

Everybody was shocked except Sanji. He found it amusing. Malik cut his eyes at him and that only made Sanji laugh even more.

Holding his hand up, Sanji tried to stop himself from laughing so he could talk.

"I'm not laughing because she was in an accident. To be honest," he said, wiping the tears from his eyes, "the shit was sad. When I got on the scene, the paramedics were putting Ailani on the stretcher and all you heard her screaming was, "I'm gon' kill you, Malik! Over and over." Sanji laughed.

"Man, look, her mama didn't lie. Ailani is off her rockers. I was the first person to approach the car. I was like, Ailani? She was smiling the whole time and she said, I'm not Ailani." Malik's eyes bulged, causing his friends to laugh. "I'm staring this woman in the eyes and she introduced herself as Christine! That's not even the kicker. She said if I got her out before the police came, she promised not to kill me! Bitch, what?"

"Damn, bro. You were definitely sleeping with the enemy for years. How the hell you didn't know she was a psycho?" Ahmad asked.

Malik thought about the question and chortled. "Ailani took vitamins every day. I had no reason to check the bottle that clearly said One a Day for women."

"Well, that's how she got away with taking the crazy pills right under your nose. Then when you didn't show back up after our trip, she stopped taking them muthafuckas." Chade laughed. "You gon' make me go to the crib checking Baylei's shit."

"So where is Ailani now?" Ahmad asked.

"They locked her ass up in a facility with padded walls. She damn near bit off the nose of one of the paramedics. She was causing hell even without the use of her damn legs. She's never getting out of that place and there's no way she will be able to escape."

That was good for all of them to hear. Malik went through a lot in the past two months when it came to Ailani and the bull crap she caused. If anyone deserved anything, Malik sure did. Ahmad was sitting quietly listening to what Malik and Sanji endured. He sighed long before adjusting himself in his seat.

"I'm sorry I haven't been there for you, Malik. I've been going through my own shit since leaving St. Thomas. Chasity really damaged a nigga and I haven't been able to deal with the hurt she put me through. I've worked long and hard to keep my mind off it all. My heart has been bleeding from the inside and I've hidden it with a smile on my face."

"Man, we didn't expect you to jump up and act like it didn't affect you. Going from being in love with the woman you thought you would grow old with, to leaving her at the altar along with a shattered heart had to be tough. What I want you to know is that we will always be here for whatever you may need. We are our brothers' keepers and nothing, and I do mean nothing, will ever come between that," Chade said to Ahmad.

"The way the truth was revealed, had to happen. I wouldn't change that shit for the world. I apologize for being the one to spring it on you, but I don't regret a minute of it."

"I don't blame anyone except myself, y'all. I should've saw the deception long before that day. Chasity played the game of charade perfectly and almost got to the finish line. Without you stepping in, I would've made the biggest mistake of my life. Thank you." Ahmad stood to his feet and raised his glass in the air. His boys followed suit. "To friendship, brotherly love, and forever. This is my new beginning. Life goes on from this day forward. I love y'all."

They threw the drinks back and tapped the glassed on the table three time. "Two guns!" they all yelled loudly.

For the rest of the afternoon, the five of them had a great time. Samir zoned out a couple times, trying to figure out how he was going to win Selena's heart again. Losing his wife was something he wasn't going to do. He was going to fight until there was no fight left in him.

Meesha

Chapter 22

Walking through Walmart in Country Club Hills, Toni was doing some much needed grocery shopping. She was on her lunch break since she was still working from home. Her mind had been going a thousand miles a minute the past couple days. Tangie hadn't made good on her promise to call or text every day and Toni had been about ready to lose her mind. She took heed to what Malik had told her and went on with her life. Going back into the office wasn't something she could do at the moment.

As Toni pushed her cart slowly down the aisle while checking things off her list. She suddenly stopped when she ran into something. Glancing up, her eyes connected with the one person she tried to avoid like a plague; LaZeric. He stood looking her body up and down and Toni tried her best to ignore the lust in his eyes.

"Antonia, nice running into here. How you been, Gorgeous?"

"Don't call me that, LaZeric. I've been fine, and enjoy the rest of your day." Toni backed the cart up and attempted to walk around his tall frame. LaZeric had other plans and stepped right into her path. "We're not about to play this game, okay? What do you want from me?"

"There isn't anything I actually want, Toni. I've taken the chance to apologize for the way I handle things between us. You have every right to be upset with me and I have to eat that shit up. The love you showed me was impeccable and it didn't go unnoticed. Your loyalty is through the roof. Toni, I just can't give you the love you deserve and that's the reason I backed away. It wasn't a lie when I told you that I loved you. I really meant that shit. It may not have seemed like it, but I promise, you have my heart."

Everything LaZeric said went in one ear and out the other. For years he'd finessed Toni into believing the love she had for him was the same love he had in return. If that was the case, the two of them would be standing tall as one, deeply in love. Instead, LaZeric was with the person he wanted to be with, but wanted Toni to wait on the sideline until he was ready to give her the unconditional love she craved.

"That's very hard to believe, but if you say so. Here's the thing, LaZeric. I know how my loyalty is set up and on top of that, I also know how hard I love. Regardless of the fact, I don't regret experiencing those two attributes with you. It did teach me a valuable lesson though. And that lesson is to not give more than I'm receiving in return. I played myself when I thought being patient was the way to finally get into your heart. That shit only broke mine; you know, the one you claimed you wouldn't hurt." Toni closed her eyes and licked her lips as she fought back tears.

"LaZeric, your decision to let me go gave me the opportunity to meet a man that's for me. Someone that puts me before all others without running from how he truly feels. We may not be in love as of today, but there is so much potential in what we are building together and I'm loving every minute of it. I'm over waiting years to be someone's number one. I want that shit from the start and I think I've found it. So, make this your last time expressing your feelings because your time has expired on that. I don't want to hear it. I have a man, LaZeric, and you got the friend you always wanted in me."

Toni pushed her cart way from LaZeric and he didn't even try to follow her. He knew deep down that she was a great woman and he lost a real one. There was nothing LaZeric could do other than let her go and be happy. Toni deserved to be truly happy and like she said, she had that. It was showing through the glow she possessed on her face. The nigga was doing her body right because that ass was thick as fuck. LaZeric shook the image out of his head, but he still saw it long after Toni rounded the corner.

Twenty minutes later, Toni was checked out and ready to get back home. She had to hurry back because her break was damn near over. Jacob had been very irritated since she hadn't been in the office and Toni didn't understand why. Her workload was still getting done in a timely manner without delays, so what was the problem? Until Jacob talked to her about the situation, she wasn't going to sweat it.

As she quickly threw her bags in the backseat of her car, Toni hoped and prayed LaZeric was long gone. Scanning the perimeter of the parking lot, she didn't see him and thanked the man upstairs. Toni got into her car and drove the five minutes to her house. Taking as many bags as she could in one trip, Toni fumbled with her keys and finally was able to unlock the door. She dropped the bags in the doorway and went out to get the rest from the car.

Her phone started ringing, but whoever it was would have to wait until she was settled inside. Toni stepped into the house and went straight to the kitchen. The phone started ringing again and she dug it out of her purse and answered it quickly.

"Hello," she said without looking to see who was on the other end.

"Toni, you need to get over here right now." Her aunt's voice was calm, but there was a slight tremble in it as well. "It's Tangie. She died, baby."

Toni heard what her aunt said, but it didn't register right away. "What did you say?" Toni asked.

"She came over last night and I sent her upstairs to sleep off whatever she was on. Tangie told me she loved me and went to lay down. When I went to check on her, she was unresponsive. I did all that I could, CPR, begging for her to breathe, but it was too late. My baby was already gone."

"I'm on my way, Auntie. This is what I was afraid of," Toni sobbed.

"She's resting now. No more pain. I want to prepare you, the police are here, but the coroner hasn't made it yet. She's still upstairs."

"I can't see her like that. I'm coming, but I'll stay outside. Just give me a minute."

Toni ended the call and sank down to the floor. The cries that escaped her body came from her soul. Tangie's face displayed behind her closed lids smiling brightly. Toni's chest heaved as she tried to catch her breath. The words 'she died, baby' echoed in her head over and over causing Toni to cover her ears to make it stop.

Her body shook uncontrollably as she fumbled to call Malik. He was the first person she wanted to hear from at that time.

"Hey, how you doing?"

"Tangie died today. My aunt just called and told me."

"Oh no, baby. I'm about to book a flight and I'll be there soon as I can. Try to be strong until I get there."

"I'm about to head to my aunt's house. My biggest fear was getting the exact phone call I just received. I tried to help her!" Toni wailed. "If I'd only did more and not let her dictate when she would keep in contact with me. I gave her space. I shouldn't have given her any lead way. This hurts so bad! It's partially my fault because I knew what the fuck was going on!"

"Toni! Toni! Please don't blame yourself. Stop crying, baby. There was nothing you could've done."

"I could've done more than what I did! The way she spoke, I knew she wanted to be reunited with my parents because she hasn't been the same since they died. She's right where she wanted to be, but she didn't take into consideration about how I would feel! Tangie, you had the opportunity to talk this shit out! I thought when we had our last heart to heart you were going to get it together."

Malik held the phone listening to Toni breakdown and he felt the hurt pouring from within. His baby was hurting and there was nothing he could do to stop it. Her cries affected him in more ways than she knew. Placing the phone on speaker, Malik found a flight and booked it quickly. He would be in Chicago in four hours tops. After getting his reservation, he went to his text messages as Toni muttered to herself.

Malik: Aye, bro. I just booked a flight to Chicago. Toni's cousin died and I need to get there. She's fucked up. Tell Baylei that Toni needs her.

Chade must've had his phone close because he responded back immediately.

Chade: WTF! Send me your flight information so I can get on the same flight. In the meantime, Toni don't need to be alone. I'm going to call Vincent so he and Chaya can go over there with her.

Malik: Tell them to go now. I'll keep her on the phone because she's trying to get herself together to go over to her aunt's house. The thing about that, Tangie's body is still in the house.

Chade: Fuck! Okay, I'm on it. Thanks for calling, bro. I'll hit you back in a minute to let you know if we got on the flight.

Malik: Okay

Malik rushed up to his room and started sifting through his clothes. He was going to have to pack quickly because he wanted to be ready to roll when the time came. Toni's voice paused his movements when she spoke softly.

"I didn't hear you. What did you say?" Malik asked.

"My boss is calling. I'll hit you right back," she said, clicking over. Before she could say anything, Jacob's voice boomed through the headset.

"Toni, why haven't you logged back in yet? Your lunch has been over. This working from home thing has gone on long enough. I'm going to need you back in the office tomorrow and also, you will be going out into the field. It's not up for debate at all. Either you do it, or find another place of employment."

Toni didn't have the strength to argue with someone that she has carried the entire time she'd worked for that damn company. She'd just been hit with a bombshell and Jacob wanted to call with some bullshit she wasn't going to entertain. Toni couldn't believe the bullshit, but it didn't put any stress on her because she didn't need the job anyway.

"Jacob, I have a lot going on in my personal life at this time," Toni said as calmly as she could.

"You've been out of the office for a month! That's more than enough time for you to get back in here and do the work you are getting paid to do," he snapped.

"Stop right there! It doesn't matter how long I've been out of the office! I haven't slacked with the work that I've done from afar!

If you really want to talk about the money I make to do my job, I should be getting half of *your* salary as well since I'm doing my job and yours! Fuck you, Jacob! Take that job and stick it up your ass! I'll be there when I feel up to it - to get my belongings and to give you the keys to that shit hole."

Toni disconnected the call and started crying all over again. She never expected Jacob to come at her the way he did. Even though she didn't keep him in the loop about what was going on in her life, she never stopped doing her job. Shaking off the anger that had built up in her, Toni put the groceries away and headed for the door. She pulled opened the door and was met by Chaya and Vincent.

"Oh my God, y'all scared me!" Toni squealed with her hand against her chest.

"Malik and Chade sent us over to make sure you're okay," Chaya said, drawing Toni into a hug. "I'm so sorry for your loss."

The gesture alone broke Toni down again. Tears cascaded down her eyes as she pulled away from Chaya. Vincent touched her shoulder and she wiped her hand across her face.

"This is the worst day of my life outside of losing my parents. This one hurts a little deeper because Tangie was my best friend, my cousin, my muthafuckin' sister. Why is this shit happening to me?" Chaya started crying with Toni and they hugged again.

"Malik told me you were going over to your aunt's," Vincent said as he stood off to the side. Toni nodded her head yes. "You don't need to be driving in the condition you're in. Come on so we can get you to your family. Malik will be here in a few hours."

Vincent led them to his car and Chaya got in the back with Toni. He followed the directions to the house and other than that, the ride was relatively quiet. When he pulled up on the block, there were so many cars and people out in the streets. Toni didn't speak of her family and Vincent didn't know she had so much support.

"You can park behind that black car," Toni said, pointing toward the house.

Getting out as soon as Vincent stopped the car, Toni walked in the direction of her aunt and they hugged while crying. A couple of her cousins consoled her as well while Vincent and Chaya looked on. They decided to just sit in the car while waiting for Toni to make her rounds with her family. The scene was so sad and Vincent found himself consoling Chaya because she was feeling the pain Toni and everyone else was feeling.

Toni kept looking at the door to the home she spent so many years in and wanted so badly to go inside. She had to use the bathroom, but she was forcing herself to avoid what was upstairs waiting to be brought out. Her aunt walked over and kissed her cheek grasping her hand.

"Come on so you can say goodbye in your own way, Toni," she said, tugging her arm gently. Tony planted her feet and stepped back, shaking her head no. "It's okay. Tangie looks like she's sleeping."

"Auntie, I can't do it. There's no way I can see her like that. Having to attend her funeral and seeing her in a casket is going to be hard enough. I'll wait until that day comes. Right now, I have to concentrate on the good times we had together. The days when she was alive and well, dressed to impress and smiling big. I'm going to miss her soooo much."

"I know, baby. We all are. Don't beat yourself up, Toni. Cry, if that's what you need to do. I'll be there every step of the way. It's hard to believe I only have one baby left; and that's you. But I will love you forever and ever; believe that. You have a lot of life to live, Toni. I want you to live it to the fullest and keep making me proud."

Toni thought about the reason she wouldn't leave Chicago and the tears flowed. Tangie was gone and there was no reason for her to stay anymore. Aunt Brenda had Uncle Rob to look after her. She, on the other hand, felt the void in her heart and knew she had to go. Not knowing how her aunt would feel about it, she decided to let her know her plans.

"Aunt Brenda, this may not be the time to tell you this, but after losing Tangie, I have no reason to stay here anymore. Malik has been asking when I would be moving to California and I didn't want to leave my cousin behind. She can enjoy the sunny skies of Cali with me and I've decided to take him up on his offer. Not to mention, I quit my job today too. Jacob called talking crazy to me right after you delivered the worst news of my life. Living here isn't an option anymore. I love you and Uncle Rob, but I won't be able to do it anymore."

"I understand, and you have to do what's best for you. Malik is a fine young man that's doing great for himself. I know you are going to be in good hands with him. Did he handle the situation with that woman?" she asked.

"Truthfully, I don't know. The only thing I know at this time, Auntie, is that I have to start over fresh. Losing my mama and daddy was a huge hit for me, but Tangie losing her life just took the cake. My heart is hollow right now and I don't know what I'm feeling. After the services, I'm leaving. But I promise, anytime you need me, I will be right here for you."

"I know you will, Toni. This will not break me. I miss my baby already and I want her back. I may have talked a lot of shit to her, but it was for her own good. I couldn't help Tangie, and you couldn't either. Tangie had to be the one to get herself out of the situation she was in. We will have to take this day by day. We will get through this together."

"We sure will. I'm going across the street to walk around the park for a little while. Standing this close to the house is doing something to me."

Aunt Brenda hugged her again before she was greeted by another family member. Toni walked across the street and just started walking the track thinking to herself. Time went by slowly in her mind, but the hours passed rapidly because before Toni realized, the sun had set and darkness surrounded her. She looked toward the house and so many people were still out. At that moment, the coroner's van pulled up and her anxiety spiked high.

Tears stung her eyes with knowing what was finally about to happen. Toni stopped where she stood and watched from afar as the workers made their way into the house. She saw her aunt go in behind them and felt bad because she wasn't strong enough to stand by her side in her time of need. Crying silently, Toni's knees gave way and she fell to the grass and held her head. The touch of someone hugging her tightly caught her attention. Blinking away the moisture, she looked up and cried as she clutched Malik's strong arms.

"I got you, baby," he said helping her to stand. "I'm here."

Hugging him tightly, she glanced under his arm just as the body of her cousin was wheeled out of the house in a black bag. The sound of her aunt's cries filled her ears as she screamed for her only child. The scene broke Toni to her core. Without Malik holding her up, she would've collapsed where she stood. Noticing Baylei and Jordyn consoling one another only made her cry even more. Toni watched the van slowly drive up the block and knew life was never going to be as she'd known it again.

Meesha

Chapter 23

Toni helped her aunt plan the celebration of Tangie's life and she was there the best she could. Having her friends by her side helped and got her through the process. Every day they gathered together with family and partied, played cards, and caught up as they reminisced about the good old days. There were always tears mixed with laughter, but they tried to keep each other's minds off what was yet to come.

The outpouring of love from people they hadn't seen in years was amazing. Many didn't know Tangie's situation but the love was shown regardless.

It was the day before the service and Toni was dreading stepping foot in the funeral home. She was laying in Malik's arms on the sofa as their friends sat scattered around wherever they could sit throughout the house.

"You need to eat, Toni," he said, stroking her hair.

"I can't. I'll make it through," Toni said, reaching over to grab the glass of pineapple Amsterdam with piña colada juice.

Malik intercepted it by taking the glass away and getting up to dispose of it. "You've had enough. Drinking isn't going to take away what's happening right now. The last thing you need is to become depended on the bottom of a bottle, Toni. I sat back and watched you indulge for the past two weeks and the consumption is getting out of control. Enough is enough."

She knew he was right and there was no way she could argue with Malik about it. The alcohol numbed all the feelings that came out on a whim. Toni got up and headed straight for her room to get some sleep. It was the next best thing to a drink and she needed to go inside the shell she'd created over the source of a couple weeks.

The service was at noon and she would need as much rest as possible to get through the day. Her clothes were already hanging in the closet. All she had to do was shower and get dressed. The previous week, she packed everything to get a head start on her move to California. Malik suggested she wait a while so she could make sure her aunt was going to be okay, but she declined.

Aunt Brenda was handling things pretty well. Toni was the one that broke when she went to the visitation earlier that day. Seeing Tangie in her white pantsuit with her hair in a laid lace frontal wig, had Toni smiling after the initial shock of seeing her lying in the powder pink casket wore off. Tangie looked like she was sleeping with a slight smile on her face.

Toni laid down in her king-sized bed and thought about the day she told Malik about her plans to leave Chicago. He was surprised she actually made the decision after everything she'd said when they were discussing it at his home. Toni filled him in on quitting her job and what happened with Jacob. Malik was ready to be there for her in any way possible, but she said there was no need because she would be alright. She found a spot for her Paralegal Services business and put an offer on the building.

Toni put ads online offering her services and also for other paralegals to come work for her. She was getting everything in order even though it felt as if her world had crashed down around her. There was no way she was moving to expensive-ass California without any money coming in for too long. She was all about stacking her money and she would make sure there was a constant flow. Going broke was never in her plans. She had money, but it wasn't enough to live off of for the rest of her life.

She'd also bought a building to open a salon. That was something Tangie always wanted to do, and now she had it. Tangie's Cuts was going to be up and running in the near future and Toni was ready to make her proud from heaven's gates.

Finally allowing her body to relax, Toni was sleeping long before Malik joined her in bed.

The next morning, everyone was up early and was ready to head out when the family car pulled up outside. Toni was taking baby steps out the door because she didn't want to say goodbye. Malik stood by her side until she was ready to face the inevitable. When the car stopped in front of the funeral home, Toni stayed put. She didn't move until her aunt opened the door and escorted her out of the car. The air smelled stale for whatever reason.

"You got this. Coming to the viewing yesterday gave you a sense of what you will endure at this moment right here. That's the reason I suggested it. Because I didn't want a repeat of what happened four years ago," Aunt Brenda said, squeezing her hand.

Toni looked down at her white pantsuit, identical to her cousin's, and took a deep breath. After a couple minutes, she was ready to get inside so she could put the painful day behind her.

Toni got through the service without shedding a single tear. She was being strong for everyone around her so the chance to cry didn't show up at all. It wasn't until they were on the way to the cemetery and out of nowhere Bone Thugs-N- Harmony's "Crossroads" blared through the speakers and tears sprang from her eyes.

Toni broke down the closer they got to the cemetery because that day would be the first time she'd been there since her parents were laid to rest. Tangie would be laid at their feet. There was no doubt that she was welcomed into heaven's gates with opened arms. The tears flowed freely until Toni heard a whisper in her ear.

"I'm good, Baby. I love you." Followed by the sound of Tangie's laugh.

Toni laughed with her cousin as the tears kept rolling from her eyes. Tangie always knew how to make her smile, and that day was no different. Toni got the confirmation she needed to move on with her cousin's spirit following her every step of the way.

Shedding tears over her mother's and father's graves after Tangie was lowered in the ground, Toni hugged both tombstones in one big hug. "I miss y'all so much. I promise not to take too long to visit again. Coming here is so hard, but I have to get out to check on my favorite people. Please take care of Tangie up there. She didn't deserve to be there, but I can't question God. I know he made a mistake when he called her home. Anyway, I love all of y'all. If there wasn't a time that I needed either of you, I need y'all now. I'm not the strong one after today. I'm so weak, and I need y'all like never before."

Everyone stood around and let Toni cry until she was exhausted. Malik scooped her up in his arms and walked to the car. Cradling her in his arms, he kissed her forehead as she snored lightly from the deep sleep she'd fallen in just that quickly. When they reached Toni's house, Malik went upstairs and placed Toni in the bed and closed the door so she could rest.

Aunt Brenda was moving food outside to the backyard when he joined everyone downstairs. Malik and his friends helped every way they could before the party started. The repast turned into a full-blown celebration and Toni slept through most of it. She eventually came out later dressed in a pair of leggings and an oversized hoodie. Brenda was finally able to get Toni to eat something.

"You finally woke up, huh?" Malik asked as he wrapped his arms around her waist from behind.

"Yeah, my body gave out on me. I didn't have a choice in the matter this time. I had a dream that me and Tangie was out having the time of our lives at a house picnic. She was dancing the whole entire time and it felt so real. We were eating Italian sausages, ribs, and them damn Hi Chew candies." Toni laughed, then sadness replaced the smile on her face immediately afterwards.

"Nope, we're not going back there. Not right now."

Malik took Toni's hand as an upbeat temple of music filled the air. Leading her to the middle of the yard, he started dancing with his woman to get her mind off Tangie no longer being with them. It worked, and Toni started having a good time. The festivities went on well into the night until everyone was tired from all the food, drinks, and dancing, they'd done. After helping with the cleanup, Toni walked her aunt and uncle to their car.

"So, you're leaving tomorrow?" Brenda asked.

"Yes. The moving company will be here to pack everything up in the morning. Malik is going to assist them because I doubt if I will be able to budge after the day I've had."

"Toni, how the hell are they supposed to move the bed if you're in it? You will have to get your tail up at some point." They laughed because Brenda was speaking nothing but truth with her statement. "I love you so much, baby. Thank you for being my rock today."

"Auntie, I don't know where my strength came from. This day will forever be etched in my mind. I love you with everything in me and I mean that. Don't hesitate to call me at any time. I will drop anything for you."

"I know. The hard part is just beginning, but it will get easier with time. Tangie can now look over the both of us at the same time. She will always live within us; in our hearts."

"That's so true. I know you're tired and need to go to sleep. I'll be over before I head to the airport. You're going to Cousin Matt's house, right?"

"No, I'm going home. I didn't get any sleep while at Matt's. Tangie's presence will forever be there and I'm ready to face it head on. She'll be walking around leaving those damn candy wrappers on the counter any day now." she chuckled. "Let me get out of here. I'll have breakfast ready for you all when you get there. Can't allow you to leave without my infamous pancakes."

Toni and her aunt hugged and didn't want to let go. "I love you to the moon and back, auntie. Stay strong, we will get through this. Be ready to come visit in two months. Tangie's Cutz Grand Opening is going to be epic!" Toni finally revealed her plans with her aunt.

"Oh wow, Toni! You always told Tangie her name would shine bright. Thank you. I'll be ready," she smiled.

Toni watched her aunt get in the car and Rob walked over and hugged her. When they pulled out of the driveway, a lone tear fell from her eye and Toni wiped it away quickly. She was going to get through the trying times no matter what. Tangie was a factor in Toni's life. That's all she needed to remember in order to push forward.

***

The movers had come in like a tornado and wiped Toni's home clean. Her car was the last thing placed on the truck before the driver pulled away, heading to California. Baylei made her move a couple weeks prior and Jordyn gave up her place as well. The three of them were ready to take on whatever the West Coast had in store for them. Toni had given all of her winter clothes to a shelter and most of her furniture to the Goodwill because she didn't need it. Plus, she wasn't going to need the heavy jackets and coats where she was headed.

"Are you ready to take this Chicago twang to Cali?" Baylei smirked.

"We'll see once I get settled. How's your transition to the new life you've embarked?"

"Well, I went into the new office and I believe it's going to be great. The staff is wonderful and I love the view I have."

"Lei, you know damn well I'm not talking about work," Toni laughed. "How's things with you and Chade?"

"Things are going very well with Mr. Oliver. There are times when we go out and one of his past troubles walks up like they are spilling tea. But babyyyyy! When he shuts their asses down and introduces me as *the wife*, it makes me so proud. Not to mention the sight of the rock that continues to weigh down my ring finger."

"Chade better let them hoes know! Girl, you walked into that man's life and made him realize that he needed a classy bitch to represent his ass. Long as he knows what he has, y'all will be alright."

"You damn right we gon' be straight," Chade said, walking into the kitchen, catching the ass end of their conversation. "There's no female that can top my baby." Kissing Baylei passionately on the lips, Chade slipped his tongue in her mouth while palming her ass.

"I'm so glad we have a plane to catch," Toni said, rolling her eyes.

"Not before we go to Aunt Brenda's. I'm hungry as hell," Baylei said, breaking the kiss.

Malik walked in followed by Sanji and Jordyn. They all laughed and talked shit for a bit before leaving Toni's home for the last time. She never thought she would leave the house her mother and father raised her in. The house would forever be in her family because Toni had no plans of selling the property. She put it up for rent everywhere she could online and found a realtor that would oversee the showings. Toni was looking forward to making a profit whenever they found someone that wanted to rent.

After dropping the keys off to the realtor's office, they went to Brenda's. Breakfast was nothing short of what Toni and her friends were used to, but Chade's hungry ass was ready to move in to keep getting good food every day. Rob told him that wasn't up for discussion and it was time for him to get out. The women laughed because they knew Rob was serious as hell.

After saying their goodbyes and hugging Toni's aunt and uncle, the group hopped in the truck and made their way to Chade's mother's house to pick up Vincent. Honking the horn once they pulled into the driveway, Capri, Chade's mom, came outside with a mug on her face.

"Chade, you know better than to be out here honking that damn horn at my house. Don't no hoes live here!"

"Come on, Ma. Pipe that down and tell Vincent we gotta go," Chade said, getting out of the truck. "He's going to make us late."

"You may have to go in and get him. Your sister doesn't deserve that man, Chade. I don't know why he insists on coming back her every other weekend to be with her. Talk to her."

Chade had no intentions of talking to anybody. He told Vincent he was too damn old to be fucking around with his sister in the first place. Chaya was still in her prime and wanted to have fun all the time. Vincent didn't like the way she partied and wanted her to move their relationship to another level. Chaya wasn't having it. She loved her life in Chicago and whenever she came to California, it was just to get away for a small amount of time.

"That's not my business, Ma. Chaya and Vincent would have to handle that on their own. I've already warned them and they didn't listen." Chade took out his phone and called Vincent. He answered, but didn't say anything to Chade.

"What's it going to be, Chaya? I don't have time to play these kiddie-ass games with you. There's nothing I've done for you that I regret, but you're standing here handling me like I'm one of these lame niggas right now."

"I didn't ask you for anything other than to let me live my life the way I see fit. I'm not trying to be a damn housewife. Why are you trying to change what we have? The relationship we've had for years has been just fine. Now you want to attempt to take me away from the only home I know."

"Grow up! I asked you what are we doing and you turn that into me asking you to move. Not one time did I make that suggestion."

"Vincent, I don't know what you want from me, but I don't want change. Look, Chade is waiting for you. I'll talk to you later," Chaya said, sitting on the bed.

Vincent shook his head and looked down at his phone. He shook his head because Chade heard their whole disagreement. Slinging the strap of his bag over his shoulder, he left the bedroom without so much as a goodbye to Chaya. Vincent kissed Capri on the cheek and bounced down the stairs. Chade approached him and Vincent held his hand up and got in the truck.

"Let Chaya know I'll hit her up later. I love you, lady." Chade hugged his mother and slipped some money into her hand. He rushed to the truck and backed out of the driveway as she yelled about the amount of money he'd left her with.

Everyone laughed because as they drove off, Capri was still screaming at the top of her lungs. Chade drowned her out by turning up the radio and the mini party began as they rode in the direction of the airport.

The entire ride, they sang karaoke style and had the time of their lives. It was something Toni needed to keep her mind off what she was leaving behind.

Chapter 24

Two months had passed since Toni moved across the country with Malik. Things were going fairly well and she had no complaints. Their relationship had grown further than she'd expected in such a short period of time. The love she received from his parents kind of filled the void of not having her mother and father around. Cookie didn't give Toni a chance to wallow in the pain she still had about losing Tangie. She made sure she was there every step of the way while Toni got Tangie's Cutz ready for opening.

The Grand Opening was set to open its doors that very day and the nervousness was showing with every tick of the clock. Toni received a call from Brenda a few days before and she couldn't make it. That alone saddened her. Then to make matters worse, Baylei and Jordyn bailed on her because both of them couldn't get out of traveling for work since the newly Boss Lady hired Jordyn to work for her.

Toni really felt as if she was being tested and just wanted to cancel the entire event, but Malik put the hype back into it all by saying the show must go on. She stood in the mirror admiring the short pink and turquoise off the shoulder dress Malik purchased for the evening. Toni loved the clear red bottom shoes with black heels that accentuated the dress very well. The tight chiffon bun that adorned her head gave the diamond choker she wore all the attention. The jewels glistened brighter than sunlight every time the light it. Her right wrist glistened just as bright with a matching bracelet.

"Yes, you are beautiful. That ass looks good and you have legs for days." Malik smiled from behind her.

Seeing Malik in the black tailored Tom Ford suit made her lady parts thump wildly in the barely there thong she wore under her dress. His tapered cut and razor-sharp lining gave her goosebumps. Toni almost said fuck the grand opening so she could jump his bones.

"You gon' get enough coming around me looking that damn good, Dr. Daniels. That shit should be against the law." Toni licked her lips seductively as she turned to face him.

"No, no, no, ma'am. We're not going there. I gave you all I had to give last night and ate you up real good this morning. That should hold you over until we make it home later tonight."

"Shid, I'm gonna have to pull you into my office so we can bless the spot. I'm not going to be able to contain myself until we get home. So get ready to rearrange my organs once I get the chance to sneak us away from the crowd."

"I see I've created a monster." Malik smirked. "I knew I shouldn't have given it to you in the booty."

Toni laughed loudly as her cheeks got hot as fire. She'd let Malik take her back door virginity and she loved every bit of it. Never in a million years did she think anal sex would be something she fell in love with. But she was so wrong. The session they had played in her mind and had her smiling brightly.

"Bring your freaky ass on. My boys are already on their way to the shop and I'm quite sure the turnout is going to be one for the books. It was a good idea to advertise your Grand Opening, babe. I'm so proud of you."

"Thank you, baby. I couldn't have pulled this off without you. I can't wait to see how you set everything up in the shop."

"Well, the wait is almost over, my love."

Malik chose all the furniture and equipment for the shop. The only thing he allowed was Toni's input about the color scheme. Other than the turquoise and pink coloring, she had no clue what she would walk into once the ribbon was cut. Grabbing her pink clutch, Toni stuffed her phone inside and left the room. She headed for the garage so they could get in the car.

"Where are you going? Our ride is already in the driveway," Malik said, motioning his hand toward the door.

Toni didn't think anything of it as her heels clicked with every step she took. Opening the door, Toni squealed with delight as she laid eyes on a brand-new midnight black Porsche 911. She wasn't one that gushed over material shit, but that was her dream car. Toni had the money to purchase the vehicle. She just didn't like spending unnecessary money on a car.

"Malik! I told you about this car in St. Thomas and I also told you why I didn't own one!"

"I understood why you didn't want to buy it. We never discussed anything about *me* buying it for you. Do you like it?"

"I love it! I can't accept this though. It's too much, baby." Toni said, walking around the car. When she made it to the front of the car, her hands flew to her mouth. Toni shook her head from side to side slowly and the tears ran down her face in doves.

"Toni, I had to do it, baby. Now you will have her rolling through the streets of Cali at all times."

Toni couldn't stop crying as she stared at the license plates, which read "Tangie1". The gesture was one that she would remember for the rest of her life. "Thank you so much! I'll never be able to top this," Toni cried as she ran into his arms.

Malik patted her face the best he could and led her to the inside of the car. In the headrests, "Tangie" was etched into each one in pink and turquois. Seeing her cousin's name again brought more tears out of Toni's eyes. Malik had gone over and beyond for her and the feelings she had for him rose several notches.

"This is so beautiful," she said, snapping a few pictures to send to Baylei, Jordyn, and her aunt. "We about to be late! Please give me a minute to touch up my makeup." Toni rushed toward the house and doubled back, "I love you so much, Mr. Daniels. You're going to get all this pussy when we get home."

Malik laughed as he watched Toni rush into the house. Pulling his phone out, he dialed Chade's number. "I just gave her the whip. We should be there in about half hour. She had to fix her makeup."

"I told you sis was going to love that shit. Everything is good to go, so just give me a heads up when y'all are close," Chade said happily. "Toni deserves all that and more. You should've told her not to worry about the makeup because she gon' fuck that shit up again."

"It's a good thing that she looks good with or without it. She'll be straight though." Malik said as Toni secured the house. "She just came out. We're heading that way now, bro."

"A'ight, bet. Get here in one piece. I'll see you soon." Chade hung up and Malik slipped his phone into his pocket.

Opening the passenger door for Toni, he went to the driver side and got in. once he started the car, "For the Love of You" by the Isley Brother's flowed through the Boise speakers.

Toni reached over and locked hands with Malik as he maneuvered her new ride onto the street. She sang the lyrics to the song while sneaking peeks at the man she found herself falling in love with more every day. When they pulled up to the salon, the crowd was gathered around the entrance. Chade stood on one side of the pink and turquois ribbon that blocked the door with a pair of pink shears in his hand.

Malik got out of the car and was greeted with smiles and pats on his back. He opened the car for Toni and the applause she received was deafening to her ears. She didn't expect to get as much love as she was receiving, but she took it all in. Her stylists were wearing customized aprons with the Tangie Cutz logo on the front. Toni didn't know anything about doing hair, but it was something Tangie loved to indulge in. One thing she did know how to do was make and manage money.

Congratulations flowed through the air as Toni made her way to the doorway of the salon. The windows were covered with pink blinds that were closed to prevent anyone from seeing inside. The anxiety Toni felt to get a glimpse of the shop was on an all-time high. Chade must've saw it because he stepped forward along with the rest of the crew.

"Today is the day that a woman I've come to love like a sister will branch into entrepreneurship. Proud is a word I can honestly use when it comes to Antonia Wade," Chade said to the crowd.

"Toni, as we call her, is the phenomenal woman Maya Angelou spoke of. Through all the trying times she has endured in the past couple months, she still rose to the occasion and didn't fold," Sanji added, making her smile big.

"A woman like Toni is full circle. Within her is the power, to create, nurture, and transform in any way imaginable. That's why we are standing here today," Ahmad said as he looked around the crowd. "This strong black woman standing before you will be around for the long haul."

The speeches were stealing Toni's heart and she couldn't stop blushing.

"Toni, you are more powerful than you know and you are beautiful just as you are. Don't ever change. The world is yours and no one can take it away from you. Everything you put your mind to will flourish. You have my support one hundred percent." Samir was the last person she expected to give her any type of praise, but she felt the sincerity in his voice.

When her uncle Rob stepped forward, Toni gasped. He and Brenda weren't supposed to be in California. An arm wrapped around her shoulder and there stood her aunt. "Toni, my baby. You knew I wasn't going to miss this day for anything in the world. You brought Tangie's name to the light and I had to be here to see the finished product," Brenda said with a smile. "Malik, I love that car! Nice job, nephew. Your parents would be proud of the woman you have become; as well as Tangie. You're going to go further in this thing call life, Toni. Continue to walk with your head held high, with grace, and dignity. As long as you believe, you will definitely concur everything in your path."

Everyone clapped loudly and Toni cried openly. Chade held the scissors out for Toni to take and took a step back. Drying her eyes, she cleared her throat wishing her two best friends would pop out like her aunt did. That was wishful thinking on her part though. When she spotted Cookie and Malik Sr., Toni beamed with happiness.

"I want to thank all of you for showing up to the opening of my salon. For all that don't know, this means so much to me because a special someone named Tangela Wade is the inspiration behind all this. Losing my cousin stifled me at first, but as the days went on, I thought of plenty of ways to give her the shine she deserves. Even though she's not here physically, she will forever watch over all that I do. This one is for you, Tangie. It's your time, baby and I love you."

Toni and Brenda cut the ribbon together and Tangie's Cutz was officially open for business. Malik led Toni inside after securing a silk turquois scarf over her eyes. She didn't even ask the question of why that danced on the tip of her tongue. Going with the flow, she just followed his lead. Once everyone was comfortably inside, Malik removed the scarf and stepped back.

The first thing Toni noticed was the hand-painted portrait of Tangie on the far wall. The caption read, "In Loving Memory of Tangie". The picture Baylei took of her the night they went out to Reynold's was the inspiration for the painting. Her makeup was ruined and Toni wouldn't have any other choice but to wash it off completely before she could take any pictures.

"Whose idea was that?" she asked, pointing.

"We did it for you, sis." Toni's head snapped in the direction she thought the voices came from. Baylei and Jordyn stepped forward with a dozen pink and turquois roses in crystal vases in hand. The trio hugged once the crowd let Toni's friends through. The tears were flowing because they all loved Tangie to death and beyond.

"Congratulations, Toni. We had to bring our girl to Cali." Baylei whispered in her ear.

"And y'all did that! Thank you, thank you, thank you!"

The DJ started the tunes of "For the Love of You" and Toni laughed because it was the second time the song was played in her presence. She loved the song and it reminded her of the love she now knew she had for Malik. Not wanting to put too much thought into her thinking, Toni stepped back from her friends and smelled the flowers she finally took from them.

At that moment, Malik walked toward her with his hand behind her back. Both Jordyn and Baylei stepped to the side as they watched his every move. Toni squinted as she tried to figure out what trick he had up his sleeve. She didn't have too long to wait when Sanji handed a microphone to Malik.

"Toni, I knew you were a different type of woman when I laid eyes on you a few months ago in St. Thomas. What I didn't know was how deep my love would grow for you. From day one, you were all about me. It was never about what I did for a living, how much money I possessed, but about Malik Daniels. What took the cake was when you stood ten toes down against the Queen herself; my mama! For her to love you as the daughter she never had, says a lot," Malik choked out.

"When I got hurt, you were right by my side helping me through the healing process. You never judged me about my past relationship, nor did you throw it in my face. Even though you fought tooth and nail to try not to love me, that shit didn't work because what we have together was destined to be. The last couple months proved that I needed you just as much as you needed me. Toni, I got you to relocate to be with me; that's not quite enough. You know I'm greedy in every aspect." Malik bit his bottom lip and Toni saw the gleam in his eyes which caused her to smile too.

"Antonia Wade, I don't want to be your boyfriend no more. I don't want to be your man." Malik smirked. "I want you to be my wife and me your husband. If it hasn't rang a bell yet," he said, dropping to one knee as he pulled his hand from behind his back. "It don't have to be today, tomorrow, or in the months to come. As long as the day presents itself, will you marry me?"

Toni was rendered speechless. The only thing she could do was shake her head yes, as Malik stood to his feet. He placed the beautiful ring on her finger and kissed her in a way he'd never done before. The DJ started playing that damn song again as the two slow danced in the middle of the salon.

"If you think this day was something, just wait until I show you exactly what I have in store. Toni, I'm going go all out when it comes to you because everything I do from here on out, will be for the love of you."

Stay tuned for Book 3:
Back At One: Samir and Selena

Submission Guideline

Submit the first three chapters of your completed manuscript to ldpsubmissions@gmail.com, subject line: Your book's title. The manuscript must be in a .doc file and sent as an attachment. Document should be in Times New Roman, double spaced and in size 12 font. Also, provide your synopsis and full contact information. If sending multiple submissions, they must each be in a separate email.

Have a story but no way to send it electronically? You can still submit to LDP/Ca$h Presents. Send in the first three chapters, written or typed, of your completed manuscript to:

LDP: Submissions Dept
Po Box 944
Stockbridge, Ga 30281

DO NOT send original manuscript. Must be a duplicate.

Provide your synopsis and a cover letter containing your full contact information.

Thanks for considering LDP and Ca$h Presents.

<u>NEW RELEASES</u>

MOB TIES 3 by SAYNOMORE
CONFESSIONS OF A GANGSTA by NICHOLAS LOCK
MURDA WAS THE CASE by ELIJAH R. FREEMAN
THE STREETS NEVER LET GO by ROBERT BAPTISTE
MOBBED UP 4 by KING RIO
AN UNFORESEEN LOVE 2 by MEESHA

An Unforeseen Love 2

STREET KINGS III

PAID IN BLOOD III

CARTEL KILLAZ IV

DOPE GODS III

Hood Rich

SINS OF A HUSTLA II

ASAD

RICH $AVAGE II

By Troublesome

YAYO V

Bred In The Game 2

S. Allen

CREAM III

By Yolanda Moore

SON OF A DOPE FIEND III

HEAVEN GOT A GHETTO II

By Renta

LOYALTY AIN'T PROMISED III

By Keith Williams

I'M NOTHING WITHOUT HIS LOVE II

SINS OF A THUG II

TO THE THUG I LOVED BEFORE II

By Monet Dragun

QUIET MONEY IV

EXTENDED CLIP III

THUG LIFE IV

By **Trai'Quan**

THE STREETS MADE ME IV

By **Larry D. Wright**

IF YOU CROSS ME ONCE II

By **Anthony Fields**

THE STREETS WILL NEVER CLOSE II

By K'ajji

HARD AND RUTHLESS III

THE BILLIONAIRE BENTLEYS II

Von Diesel

KILLA KOUNTY II

By Khufu

MONEY GAME II

By Smoove Dolla

A GANGSTA'S KARMA II

By FLAME

JACK BOYZ VERSUS DOPE BOYZ

By Romell Tukes

MOB TIES IV

By SayNoMore

MURDA WAS THE CASE II

Elijah R. Freeman

THE STREETS NEVER LET GO II

By Robert Baptiste

AN UNFORESEEN LOVE III

By **Meesha**

Available Now

RESTRAINING ORDER **I & II**

An Unforeseen Love 2

By **CA$H & Coffee**

LOVE KNOWS NO BOUNDARIES **I II & III**

By **Coffee**

RAISED AS A GOON I, II, III & IV

BRED BY THE SLUMS I, II, III

BLAST FOR ME I & II

ROTTEN TO THE CORE I II III

A BRONX TALE I, II, III

DUFFLE BAG CARTEL I II III IV V VI

HEARTLESS GOON I II III IV V

A SAVAGE DOPEBOY I II

DRUG LORDS I II III

CUTTHROAT MAFIA I II

KING OF THE TRENCHES

By **Ghost**

LAY IT DOWN **I & II**

LAST OF A DYING BREED I II

BLOOD STAINS OF A SHOTTA I & II III

By **Jamaica**

LOYAL TO THE GAME I II III

LIFE OF SIN I, II III

By **TJ & Jelissa**

BLOODY COMMAS I & II

SKI MASK CARTEL I II & III

KING OF NEW YORK I II,III IV V

RISE TO POWER I II III

COKE KINGS I II III IV

BORN HEARTLESS I II III IV

KING OF THE TRAP I II

By **T.J. Edwards**

IF LOVING HIM IS WRONG…I & II

LOVE ME EVEN WHEN IT HURTS I II III

By **Jelissa**

WHEN THE STREETS CLAP BACK I & II III

THE HEART OF A SAVAGE I II III

By **Jibril Williams**

A DISTINGUISHED THUG STOLE MY HEART I II & III

LOVE SHOULDN'T HURT I II III IV

RENEGADE BOYS I II III IV

PAID IN KARMA I II III

SAVAGE STORMS I II

AN UNFORESEEN LOVE I II

By **Meesha**

A GANGSTER'S CODE I &, II III

A GANGSTER'S SYN I II III

THE SAVAGE LIFE I II III

CHAINED TO THE STREETS I II III

BLOOD ON THE MONEY I II III

By **J-Blunt**

PUSH IT TO THE LIMIT

By **Bre' Hayes**

BLOOD OF A BOSS **I, II, III, IV, V**

SHADOWS OF THE GAME

TRAP BASTARD

By **Askari**

THE STREETS BLEED MURDER **I, II & III**

THE HEART OF A GANGSTA I II& III

By **Jerry Jackson**

CUM FOR ME I II III IV V VI VII

An **LDP Erotica Collaboration**

BRIDE OF A HUSTLA **I II & II**

THE FETTI GIRLS **I, II& III**

CORRUPTED BY A GANGSTA I, II III, IV

BLINDED BY HIS LOVE

THE PRICE YOU PAY FOR LOVE I, II ,III

DOPE GIRL MAGIC I II III

By **Destiny Skai**

WHEN A GOOD GIRL GOES BAD

By **Adrienne**

THE COST OF LOYALTY I II III

By Kweli

A GANGSTER'S REVENGE **I II III & IV**

THE BOSS MAN'S DAUGHTERS I II III IV V

A SAVAGE LOVE **I & II**

BAE BELONGS TO ME I II

A HUSTLER'S DECEIT I, II, III

WHAT BAD BITCHES DO I, II, III

SOUL OF A MONSTER I II III

KILL ZONE

A DOPE BOY'S QUEEN I II III

By **Aryanna**

A KINGPIN'S AMBITON

A KINGPIN'S AMBITION **II**

I MURDER FOR THE DOUGH

By **Ambitious**

TRUE SAVAGE I II III IV V VI VII

DOPE BOY MAGIC I, II, III

MIDNIGHT CARTEL I II III

CITY OF KINGZ I II

NIGHTMARE ON SILENT AVE

Meesha

By **Chris Green**

A DOPEBOY'S PRAYER

By **Eddie "Wolf" Lee**

THE KING CARTEL **I, II & III**

By **Frank Gresham**

THESE NIGGAS AIN'T LOYAL **I, II & III**

By **Nikki Tee**

GANGSTA SHYT **I II &III**

By **CATO**

THE ULTIMATE BETRAYAL

By **Phoenix**

BOSS'N UP **I , II & III**

By **Royal Nicole**

I LOVE YOU TO DEATH

By **Destiny J**

I RIDE FOR MY HITTA

I STILL RIDE FOR MY HITTA

By **Misty Holt**

LOVE & CHASIN' PAPER

By **Qay Crockett**

TO DIE IN VAIN

SINS OF A HUSTLA

By **ASAD**

BROOKLYN HUSTLAZ

By **Boogsy Morina**

BROOKLYN ON LOCK I & II

By **Sonovia**

GANGSTA CITY

By **Teddy Duke**

A DRUG KING AND HIS DIAMOND I & II III

A DOPEMAN'S RICHES

HER MAN, MINE'S TOO I, II

CASH MONEY HO'S

THE WIFEY I USED TO BE I II

By Nicole Goosby

TRAPHOUSE KING **I II & III**

KINGPIN KILLAZ I II III

STREET KINGS I II

PAID IN BLOOD **I II**

CARTEL KILLAZ I II III

DOPE GODS I II

By **Hood Rich**

LIPSTICK KILLAH **I, II, III**

CRIME OF PASSION I II & III

FRIEND OR FOE I II III

By **Mimi**

STEADY MOBBN' **I, II, III**

THE STREETS STAINED MY SOUL I II

By **Marcellus Allen**

WHO SHOT YA **I, II, III**

SON OF A DOPE FIEND I II

HEAVEN GOT A GHETTO

Renta

GORILLAZ IN THE BAY **I II III IV**

TEARS OF A GANGSTA I II

3X KRAZY I II

DE'KARI

TRIGGADALE I II III

MURDAROBER WAS THE CASE

Elijah R. Freeman

Meesha

GOD BLESS THE TRAPPERS I, II, III
THESE SCANDALOUS STREETS I, II, III
FEAR MY GANGSTA I, II, III IV, V
THESE STREETS DON'T LOVE NOBODY I, II
BURY ME A G I, II, III, IV, V
A GANGSTA'S EMPIRE I, II, III, IV
THE DOPEMAN'S BODYGAURD I II
THE REALEST KILLAZ I II III
THE LAST OF THE OGS I II III

Tranay Adams

THE STREETS ARE CALLING

Duquie Wilson

MARRIED TO A BOSS I II III

By Destiny Skai & Chris Green

KINGZ OF THE GAME I II III IV V

Playa Ray

SLAUGHTER GANG I II III
RUTHLESS HEART I II III

By Willie Slaughter

FUK SHYT

By Blakk Diamond

DON'T F#CK WITH MY HEART I II

By Linnea

ADDICTED TO THE DRAMA I II III
IN THE ARM OF HIS BOSS II

By Jamila

YAYO I II III IV
A SHOOTER'S AMBITION I II
BRED IN THE GAME

By S. Allen

TRAP GOD I II III

RICH $AVAGE

By Troublesome

FOREVER GANGSTA

GLOCKS ON SATIN SHEETS I II

By Adrian Dulan

TOE TAGZ I II III

LEVELS TO THIS SHYT I II

By Ah'Million

KINGPIN DREAMS I II III

By Paper Boi Rari

CONFESSIONS OF A GANGSTA I II III IV

By Nicholas Lock

I'M NOTHING WITHOUT HIS LOVE

SINS OF A THUG

TO THE THUG I LOVED BEFORE

By Monet Dragun

CAUGHT UP IN THE LIFE I II III

THE STREETS NEVER LET GO

By Robert Baptiste

NEW TO THE GAME I II III

MONEY, MURDER & MEMORIES I II III

By **Malik D. Rice**

LIFE OF A SAVAGE I II III

A GANGSTA'S QUR'AN I II III

MURDA SEASON I II III

GANGLAND CARTEL I II III

CHI'RAQ GANGSTAS I II III

KILLERS ON ELM STREET I II III

JACK BOYZ N DA BRONX I II III

Meesha

A DOPEBOY'S DREAM
By **Romell Tukes**
LOYALTY AIN'T PROMISED I II
By Keith Williams
QUIET MONEY I II III
THUG LIFE I II III
EXTENDED CLIP I II
By **Trai'Quan**
THE STREETS MADE ME I II III
By **Larry D. Wright**
THE ULTIMATE SACRIFICE I, II, III, IV, V, VI
KHADIFI
IF YOU CROSS ME ONCE
ANGEL I II
IN THE BLINK OF AN EYE
By **Anthony Fields**
THE LIFE OF A HOOD STAR
By Ca$h & Rashia Wilson
THE STREETS WILL NEVER CLOSE
By K'ajji
CREAM I II
By Yolanda Moore
NIGHTMARES OF A HUSTLA I II III
By King Dream
CONCRETE KILLA I II
By Kingpen
HARD AND RUTHLESS I II
MOB TOWN 251
THE BILLIONAIRE BENTLEYS
By Von Diesel

GHOST MOB

Stilloan Robinson

MOB TIES I II III

By SayNoMore

BODYMORE MURDERLAND I II III

By Delmont Player

FOR THE LOVE OF A BOSS

By C. D. Blue

MOBBED UP I II III IV

By King Rio

KILLA KOUNTY

By Khufu

MONEY GAME

By Smoove Dolla

A GANGSTA'S KARMA

By FLAME

<u>BOOKS BY LDP'S CEO, CA$H</u>

<u>TRUST IN NO MAN</u>

<u>TRUST IN NO MAN 2</u>

<u>TRUST IN NO MAN 3</u>

<u>BONDED BY BLOOD</u>

<u>SHORTY GOT A THUG</u>

<u>THUGS CRY</u>

<u>THUGS CRY 2</u>

<u>THUGS CRY 3</u>

<u>TRUST NO BITCH</u>

<u>TRUST NO BITCH 2</u>

<u>TRUST NO BITCH 3</u>

<u>TIL MY CASKET DROPS</u>

<u>RESTRAINING ORDER</u>

<u>RESTRAINING ORDER 2</u>

<u>IN LOVE WITH A CONVICT</u>

<u>LIFE OF A HOOD STAR</u>

An Unforeseen Love 2